The Lit Ones

A Vampyre Tale

Matt Sauls

Acknowledgment

The Vampyre

John William Polidori

Year: 1819

Contents

Chapter 1

"Those not busy being born are busy dying."

-Bob Dylan

Centuries. An eternity locked in the suffocating abyss of stone.

The thick and stagnant air held the weight of forgotten prayers and whispered pleas. Scratching, a sound lost to time, echoed within the confines of the sarcophagus.

It had been a symphony of desperation for a while, then a frantic clawing, and finally, just... silence.

One day, something shifted, monumental and so tiny. A sliver of light pierced the darkness. It was a pinprick at first, then a hesitant gash, growing wider until the lid creaked open, revealing a skeletal hand, long, pale fingers like petrified branches reaching for the long-forgotten sun. The hand trembled, then stilled.

Had the struggle finally ended?

Something stirred within the skeletal remains, a faint tremor that hinted at a spark of life refusing to be extinguished.

His breath hitched. In that moment, the silence that had stretched for centuries shattered. A ragged and weak gasp escaped the darkness, a sound that resonated with the weight of a thousand forgotten sunrises.

He was a being of essence, his form wispy and insubstantial.

He had been reduced to a shadow.

A faint smudge of dust clinging to the forgotten corners of his sarcophagus. The first tendrils of dawn, a pale, tentative light, crept through the cracked lid, painting the chamber in an ethereal glow. He remained unnoticed, like an insignificant speck against the vast canvas of stone.

It was a primal urge and a desperate yearning to break free from the confines of his deathbed. As the light intensified, so did the faint tendrils of his being.

He propelled himself out of the casket with a silent surge of will. He moved not with limbs but with the shadows' flow, a formless entity slipping through the cracks and crevices of the ancient chamber.

The question of who had opened the lid echoed in the emptiness, a question for later.

His sole focus, his burning purpose, was the sliver of light beckoning from beyond the confines of his stone prison. In the wisp of forgotten life, he ached to bask in the sun's embrace once more.

His shadow form coalesced, hesitantly reaching out to take in the unfamiliar surroundings. Two dim standing lamps cast an uneven glow, illuminating a vast room filled with the whispers of history.

Ancient farming tools and corroded weapons hung on massive wooden shelves. Their stories were lost to time. Giant wooden wheels leaned against the far wall, their worn spokes hinting at journeys long past. A rusted anchor, a monument to voyages never completed, stood sentinel in the corner.

A wave of realization washed over him. He was in a museum, in the very heart of its archives. The silence was profound, broken only by the faint hum of distant city life filtering through the thick walls. He was alone, a solitary shadow amidst a sea of forgotten objects, each holding secrets waiting to be unraveled. His eyes wandered around in hopes of finding his origin.

He wasn't like the others, the creatures of the night who craved the warmth of blood. His thirst was different, a yearning for the sun's vital kiss.

His sustenance was drawn from the very start that gave life to the world. The moon and other celestial bodies offered meager sustenance; mere sips compared to the sun's life-giving banquet. But the dim glow of the museum lamps, despite their warmth, did nothing to alleviate his gnawing hunger.

He needed the sun, which was the true source of his power.

The sun's rays peeked through the cracks in the mausoleum's ceiling. Long cracks snaked across the dusty surface like desperate pleas. Through the gaping wounds, slivers of sunlight speared down, not in bold, life-giving beams, but in pathetic, hesitant fingers. His hands were like the weak, trembling claws of a starving beast, desperately reaching for a scrap of food. The touch of the meager light, filtered through the cracks, was a mere caress. It felt like a whisper against the vast hunger gnawing at his being.

He was a paradox, a creature stuck somewhere between darkness and light, a shadow holding the faintest glimmer of luminescence within it. He was yearning for the sun's full embrace. It held the key not just to his physical form but to his very soul.

A jolt of energy ripped through him. His reenergizing process is erratic, marked by bursts of searing energy that are both agonizing and ecstatic. It was a forgotten language that his being desperately tried to decipher. It was a brutal baptism, a stripping away of the darkness that had become his prison.

Slowly, excruciatingly, form began to emerge from the writhing shadow. A flicker of color, a hint of definition, bloomed where only darkness resided moments before. The pain was a white-hot inferno, yet he pressed on, his essence yearning for the sun's touch.

With each agonizing moment, the sun's power grew, pushing him closer to the precipice of transformation. The being he once was fought to emerge from the ashes. The lines of his form sharpened, the muted colors gaining vibrancy. He was far from his full glory, but the sun's kiss had ignited a spark within him.

With each breath, he was becoming a being of light, forever marked by the darkness he had overcome.

The sun assaulted his senses. His blurry and unfamiliar vision struggled to make sense of the scene before him. He realized with a jolt that the museum itself seemed ancient, a relic from a bygone era.

His head spun a whirlwind of disorientation as his senses overloaded. The cacophony of a waking city shattered centuries of silence. Eons of darkness challenged by the blinding brilliance of the sun.

Light vampires, they called them. An anomaly, an enigma. Unkillable in their shadow form, they exist on the fringes of darkness and light. He was one such enigma, standing on the precipice of a forgotten life. Time, a concept once meaningless, now loomed heavy.

'How long had I slumbered? How much had the world changed?'

He had no answers, only the burning hunger for survival and the sun's power coursing through his veins.

As the day unfolded, the world around him sharpened into focus. Like shards of glass reflecting sunlight, fragments of memory began to pierce the veil of his forgotten past. A single word resonated within him: Ka. Not just a word but a concept, a key unlocking the forgotten chambers of his mind.

The Ka sword is a tangible manifestation of his spirit, a blade forged from the essence of his being. He could feel its absence, a phantom limb aching for its return. He focused, searching for the sword's energy, a faint echo across the vast distance. It wasn't destroyed, that much he knew. But it was far, far away.

Two words surfaced, intertwined with Ka-Mer and Ba. Mer, meaning light. Ba, meaning body. Together, they formed a single entity: Merkaba. It resonated deep within him, symbolizing his true self, a melding of light, spirit, and body. It was his higher self, his connection to something greater than the shadow he once was.

A wave of frustration washed over him. But the memory of the sword, a symbol of his former power, also ignited a spark of hope. He would find it. He had to. It was a piece of himself, a reminder of who he once was, and a key to who he would become in this unfamiliar world.

As the sun climbed its zenith, bathing him in its direct, invigorating rays, he finally grasped the passage of time. Hours had bled into one another, a disorienting blur since his escape from the sarcophagus. With each passing moment, the world sharpened into focus. He felt the sun's warmth on his skin and, within his very being, a divine presence he recognized as Ra, the sun god.

His weakened senses, dulled by centuries of slumber, were slowly awakening. He could smell the faint tang of exhaust fumes, hear the distant hum of traffic, and even feel the subtle vibrations of the earth beneath his feet. He was regaining his abilities, one by one.

But amidst the sense of renewal, a prickling sensation arose – a presence not unlike his. He wasn't alone. Other light vampires like him existed in this world, hidden amongst the shadows. A surge of both excitement and apprehension coursed through him.

'Were they allies or adversaries?'

He focused, sending out a tentative pulse, an echo of his being, seeking a connection, a beacon in the urban jungle.

When it came, the response was faint, a whisper in his mind, a flicker of recognition across the vast city. Three. He sensed three others, their energies faint but undeniably present.

'Where?' the answer remained elusive, a mystery waiting to be unraveled.

As the sun dipped further, casting the world in hues of twilight, his "organs" of dust buzzed with renewed energy. A feeling, a sensation, washed over him.

Three had arrived.

He felt their potent and ancient energy nearly overwhelming him in its raw intensity. Then, as abruptly as they appeared, the cloud coalesced, revealing three distinct figures, each radiating an ethereal glow. They were magnificent beings draped in garments that shimmered like moonlight on water.

"We have heard you, brother," one of them spoke, their voice a harmonious blend of whispers and chimes. "We have come to your aid."

One, a woman cloaked in shimmering light, stepped forward, her voice a melody of whispers and chimes.

"We are honored to be here with you," she said, her words imbued with a deep and resonant power. "I am Analee, princess of the southern horizon."

As she spoke, she extended a hand, revealing a fossilized snakehead, its once vibrant colors bleached by time. He hesitantly reached out, his touch sending a jolt through his form. Suddenly, a blinding flash engulfed him, followed by a wave of memories crashing down.

The bone hummed with forgotten knowledge, whispering his name – Rye.

"You are Rye," it spoke, its voice echoing from within. "Rye of the snakes."

A shudder ran through him as images flooded his mind. Ammit, the devourer, was consumed by darkness, sealing him away with an unbreakable hex. He had been forgotten, hidden from sight and memory, a prisoner in his tomb.

"She feared your power," Analee continued her voice a soothing balm amidst the storm within him. "You were hidden so no one could sense you, not even your kind."

Rye stumbled back. The weight of his lost past was pressing down on him. He sat on his knees and clutched the fossilized snakehead, a tangible link to his forgotten identity.

'Who am I? What power did I possess that Ammit so feared? And how can I reclaim my rightful place in this world?'

Analee uttered, "Eventually, after what seemed like ages, your sarcophagus was found. But no being, no matter their power, could break the concrete bonds or shatter the hex that bound you within. It was an enchantment of immense strength, designed to ensure your eternal slumber."

A flicker of surprise crossed her ethereal face.

"We were unsure if you would ever be uncovered. Then, on this day, Rye, we have found you alive. It is October, 2023."

The words echoed within him. Each syllable sounded like a piece of a forgotten puzzle finally clicking into place.

"And you are in Alexandria," she added, her voice gentle as she observed his silent struggle to process the deluge of information.

Rye reeled. Home. He had been awakened at home! Over five hundred and sixty years had passed since the darkness had claimed him. Since the year 1461, it had bled into a forgotten memory.

"We understand this is a lot to absorb," Analee continued, her voice laced with empathy. "There are others who wish to meet you, to welcome you back. But for now, rest, and do not be afraid."

The prince, his voice echoing with awe, offered their final words.

"The princess and I will leave you for now, sir, but only for a time. We will share the joyous news of your return with all of our kind. In the meantime, we recommend you soak up as much sun as you can. We are honored and amazed to have found you, Rye. Welcome back to the world."

The three light vampires shimmered with these words, their forms dissolving into wisps of ethereal mist. They faded through the air, leaving behind only the faintest scent of ozone and a lingering sense of wonder.

Rye remained on his knees, the fossilized snakehead clutched tightly in his hand. The weight of the revelation pressed upon him, a bittersweet concoction of relief and overwhelming curiosity. Centuries had passed, and the world had changed in ways he couldn't begin to comprehend. Yet, amidst the overwhelming uncertainty, a single truth burned bright: he was home.

Rye stared into the fiery heart of the sun; his eyes unflinching. Unlike humans, who flinched away from its brilliance, he absorbed the light, a nourishing feast. He pondered Analee's words – "soak up as much sun as you can."

'Was it simply to recharge, or was there more to it? Did my strength, my very being, depend on the sun's constant caress?'

He thought back to his entombment, the suffocating darkness, and a new understanding dawned.

'Humans blinked; their vision fragmented by those fleeting moments of darkness. But what if those blinks are missed opportunities for a creature like me? By keeping my eyes open, could I absorb, see, and become more?'

Closing his eyes wasn't for sleep, not anymore. Now, it was a gateway, a key to unlock the hidden worlds within. With eyes shut, fueled by the sun's bounty, his mind delved into the abyss. Images flickered, memories sharp and terrifying. Ammit, the monster dark queen, loomed large – a grotesque fusion of crocodile, lion, and hippopotamus, her eyes blazing with malevolent hunger.

She was the one who had sealed him away, the devourer who feasted on souls and unleashed darkness upon the Earth. Her mindless followers, their hearts consumed by blackness, swarmed at her command. Rye clenched his fist around the fossilized snakehead, a surge of anger coursing through him.

He remembered the battle, the desperate struggle against Ammit and her horde. He remembered the blinding flash, the searing pain, and then...nothingness—centuries of oblivion. But now, Rye of the Snakes, the light vampire, was back. He had no intentions to rest until the Crocodilian Queen had been stopped and the invisible balance between dark and lightness was restored.

Rye opened his eyes, the sun's brilliance even sharper now. He may have been awakened by chance, but his purpose was clear. Ammit, the devourer, still walked the Earth. And Rye of the Snakes, the light vampire reborn, would not rest until he had stopped her and restored balance to the world.

***

In the times of ancient Egypt, whispers of defiance flickered amongst the people. Rumblings of rebellion, challenging the very authority of the gods, reached the celestial ears. In response, Sekhmet, the lion-headed goddess, descended upon the land, her fiery gaze blazing with wrath.

With unstoppable ferocity, she tore through the ranks of the rebels, her form a whirlwind of fangs and claws. But as her rage deepened, so did her thirst for blood. Each life claimed fueled her fury, pushing her further into a bloodthirsty frenzy.

Witnessing the carnage unfold, the other deities grew alarmed. Sekhmet's wrath, intended to quell the rebellion, threatened to consume humanity itself. They devised a cunning plan. Vast quantities of beer were brewed, then painstakingly stained a deep red with ochre pigment, mimicking the hue of blood.

Drunk on the illusion and her insatiable desire, Sekhmet devoured the crimson concoction, each barrel deepening her stupor. Soon, overcome by the potent mixture, she collapsed into a deep slumber, her rampage mercifully halted.

As Sekhmet's slumber waned, she awoke to find Hathor, the goddess of love and beauty, by her side. Shame washed over the warrior goddess as she realized the devastating consequences of her rage. Then, under Hathor's gentle guidance, Sekhmet vowed never again to allow her fury to consume her.

In a gesture of redemption and transformation, Hathor integrated an aspect of Sekhmet within herself, merging the warrior's power with the nurturer's compassion. This act of divine fusion didn't diminish Sekhmet's existence but rather redirected her power toward a new purpose.

Three distinct groups, each called pods of celestial beings, emerged from this union. These were the "sunlighted ones," also known as light vampires. There were three pods created. Each pod contained three people, totaling nine individuals. They were created as fully formed male or female adults, each bearing the combined legacy of Sekhmet's strength and Hathor's gentleness.

Despite his weakened state, the remnants of Sekhmet and Hathor's guiding light flickered within him, a faint ember amidst the turmoil. He closed his eyes, focusing on that spark, channeling his will into a silent plea.

"Be my guide in this jumbled, mixed-up world," Rye implored, his voice a mere whisper against the noise of unfamiliar sensations.

His shadow form, a constant companion for centuries, felt alien now, a borrowed cloak ill-suited to his reawakened essence. He felt surges, ripples within his being, an unfamiliar hum that replaced the suffocating silence of his tomb. Even his breath, once taken for granted, held a novelty bordering on the surreal.

As he stretched and moved, the limitations of his shadow form became painfully apparent. Unlike humans, he lacked the need for sustenance in the traditional sense. His true sustenance came from the sun. Yet, the absence of a physical body was a constant reminder of his incomplete state.

He could feel the desert wind, hot and dry, whispering stories of his ancient homeland. And then, a change. A faint glow emanated from his chest, a beacon of his own making. It wasn't the blinding brilliance of the sun but a gentle luminescence radiating from his very core.

Now, back to 2023, he closed his eyes, focusing on that spark.

Rye, fueled by the dawning light within and the unwavering guidance of his celestial patrons, steeled his resolve. He wouldn't delay. He would reclaim his body, piece by piece, until he stood not just as a shadow but as a complete being, a light vampire reborn, ready to face the challenges that awaited him in this strange, new world.

His journey had begun, and he would walk it with the unwavering glow of his inner light leading the way.

Chapter 2

A surge of ancient power pulsed through Rye's veins like a forgotten language whispered in the very essence of his being. It was the blood of countless generations, a powerful cocktail of magic and mortality, stirring awake after a millennia-long slumber. He could feel it coursing through his form, each beat of his reawakened heart echoing like a drumbeat against the silence of his tomb.

Then, a pressure blossomed between his brows, a slow, inexorable unfurling. It was like a bud on the verge of blooming, pushing against its confines. He focused on the sensation, willing it open, and with a sensation like a crack of thunder splitting a silent sky, his third eye opened.

A universe unfolded behind his eyelid. It was a glimpse into reality, a language whispered in the flow of raw magic.

But amidst this celestial spectacle, a more grounded sensation anchored him. He felt it along his spine - a coiling, awakening presence. His snakes. They pulsed with renewed energy, their scales shimmering with an otherworldly glow as they slowly ascended his spine, their path marked by a trail of light.

The vibrant colors within his shadow form intensified, reflecting the turmoil within. Then, a flash. An image of Ammit's grotesque crocodilian face burned into his mind. Her voice, a raspy hiss, slithered into his thoughts, laden with both challenge and a hint of desperation.

"I know you have awoken," she transmitted telepathically. "Will you meet me on neutral grounds?"

The telepathic message hung in the air. Overwhelmed by the deluge of sensations, Rye could only grip this single thought, this tendril of awareness stretching out into the vast unknown.

He was awake.

The awakening stirred a memory, a deep, primal echo of the past. The dance. It had begun eons ago, a cosmic ballet between light and dark. Now, the music swelled anew, the melody both familiar and terrifying.

Rye, barely able to grasp the tendrils of telepathy, managed a single thought, a defiant echo in the vast emptiness.

"Who dictates the stage?"

A reply slithered into his mind, Ammit's voice a rasp that sent shivers down his resurrected spine.

"The Overseers," she hissed.

He recognized the reference. The Ennead, the ancient of ancients, judges both fair and final. They had watched over the epic clashes of Horus and Set, their pronouncements echoing through the ages.

"Then I agree," Rye replied, a steely resolve forming in his reawakened spirit.

This dance, he knew, wouldn't be a waltz. It would be a brutal war dance, a clash of wills that could shake the very foundations of reality. His solitary existence as a hermit was about to be shed. Rye, the vessel, felt himself filling with a dynamic energy, nearing its brim. Nine by nine, the equation resonated within him, a cryptic message hinting at his metamorphosis. The magus, the wielder of light, was stirring awake, ready to take its place in the cosmic dance.

"Two days," he rasped, his voice raw from disuse. It was a promise, a declaration to the entity on the other end of the telepathic connection.

"Agreed," came the reply, a hint of something akin to respect in Ammit's voice.

As the connection severed, Rye felt the weight of his solitude lift. He wasn't just a lone player anymore; he was a counterpoint to a powerful force. Here, in this desolate chamber, two demigods, born from opposing ends of the spectrum, had just made a pact.

This wasn't about brute force, about crushing darkness beneath a heel. No, the objective was far more nuanced. It was about peeling back the layers of darkness, one by one, revealing the flicker of light that might lie dormant within. It was about transmutation, a process of elevating the darkness to a higher frequency, where it could no longer cause harm.

This was the mission, the very reason Rye had chosen this path. He was destined to perform this dance, a dance between destruction and redemption.

The emerald glow emanating from his heart intensified, spreading like a luminous cloak around him. It was his aura, a shield forged from within. As the light bloomed outward, a wave of emotion washed over him - a pang for the trials his heart had endured, the sheer brutality of his entombment.

But the pain was eclipsed by a surging power. He felt the familiar slithering sensation - his spirit guides, Riven and Vipen, were coursing through him like living ropes. They reached his arms and hands, enhancing his very essence, his dance with the unseen forces of the world.

The sensation intensified as the serpents pushed upwards. They writhed in his throat as he exhaled a reverent word: "Asir," a call to the ever-present god, Osiris. With a final surge, they shot into his mind, weaving intricate patterns - light codes, perhaps - that shifted and pulsed as their size changed. A clear and powerful vision flooded his consciousness: the Ankh, the symbol of eternal life.

Rye gasped, confused by the influx of power and knowledge. It was an awakening unlike anything he'd ever known. He was no longer just Rye, the solitary vampire. He was a conduit, a vessel brimming with potential, ready to play his part in the grand cosmic dance.

A colossal yank tore through Rye as his serpents, Riven and Vipen, erupted from the crown of his head. A pillar of light, blindingly white, shot skyward, a beacon reaching out to the unknowable entities beyond. His entire being pulsed with an otherworldly luminescence, a living prism radiating raw power.

Under the watchful gaze of Ra, the most extraordinary transformation unfolded. With a rippling sensation, his physical form coalesced, separating from the shadow self that had been his only companion for so long. Now bereft of its animating force, the shadow settled back onto the wall, a silent echo of his former existence.

Rye reveled in the glorious sensation of a restored body. It felt pristine, a perfect replica of his original form. His vision, now imbued with vampiric essence, stretched far beyond human limitations. The world shimmered in a thousand shades of grey, every minute detail etched with an unfathomable clarity. He flexed his arm, marveling at the sight of flesh – his flesh, a rich brown that sent a jolt of wonder through him. It was a simple thing, this arm, yet in that moment, it held the profound miracle of life itself.

Captivated, Rye traced the lines of his hands and feet, marveling at the tangible reality of his flesh. He was whole again, a complete being bathed in the golden light of dawn. But a single element was missing. With a thought, a simple linen tunic, a thawb, materialized around his body, accompanied by a pair of sturdy sandals. The sensation of clothes against his skin was refreshingly familiar, a grounding reminder of his physical existence.

A wave of elation washed over him. He was alive. His senses buzzed with a renewed appreciation for the world, not just existing but truly alive. He basked in the rising sun's warmth, its life-giving energy soaking into his very core.

Empowered and eager, Rye reached out to his Egyptian guides. Sekhmet, the fierce lion-headed goddess, and Horus, the falcon warrior. Thoth, the wise scribe; Isis, the embodiment of magic and healing; and Osiris, the lord of the underworld – their names echoed in his mind, and he asked a silent prayer for their guidance. He stood poised on the precipice of his new reality, a resurrected warrior ready to face the dance that awaited.

A tremor ran through the air, a ripple of recognition. Osiris, the lord of the underworld, the first mummy, the god of death, resurrection, and life itself, answered Rye's call. His voice, a deep rumble that echoed through the chamber, resonated with warmth.

"We hear you, Rye. We are so pleased that you have returned. We will never leave you. We never left you."

Gratitude flooded Rye.

Memories, fragmented and hazy, flickered at the edges of his mind. He reached out, trying to grasp them and to piece together the itinerary of his past life. Images of times spent with these celestial beings surfaced - laughter shared, battles fought, wisdom imparted flitted through his mind. He transmitted a surge of gratitude, a silent thank you for their unwavering presence.

Isis, the goddess of magic, healing, and wisdom, Osiris's radiant consort, stepped forward next. Her voice, melodic and strong, soothed the turmoil within him.

"You do not walk alone, Rye. We will help you remember who you are. We know you were in a damaged, unconscious state for a long time, utter trauma, and you must know how our hearts are moved for you. You chose the narrow path, and we honor your resolve."

A powerful presence surged forward. Sekhmet, the lion-headed goddess of war and healing, the progenitor of all vampires, addressed Rye with a voice that resonated with both fierce power and nurturing warmth.

"Our son," she boomed, the sound echoing through the chamber. "You are a distinction among vampires."

Her words struck Rye with a jolt.

'Distinction? What did that mean?'

Sekhmet continued, her voice dropping to a low growl.

"Set has taken control. He's twisted Ammit and warped her into a demonic shell of her former self. She was the one who sealed you away, Rye. Yet, paradoxically, she was also the one who opened your sarcophagus. Now, with your awakening, the hex that bound you is finally shattered."

Rye's mind reeled.

'Ammit, the one who imprisoned me, is also my liberator?'

The revelation sent a wave of confusion crashing over him.

"Ammit was once a goddess," Rye murmured, piecing together the fragments of information. "No wonder the hex held so tight and gave them the power to keep the other gods at bay. Now I understand. Now I truly know."

A flicker of determination ignited in his eyes.

"Set wants the Ka sword, doesn't he?" he pressed. "They need me to get it for them, is that right?"

Horus, the falcon-headed god and national hero of Egypt, boomed a confirmation.

"That is correct, Rye. Set's hunger for chaos and destruction remains insatiable. So far, the world remains blissfully unaware of Set and Ammit's machinations, their very existence a secret on this plane."

His voice echoed with concern as he continued.

"Rye, their plan revolves around mass sacrifices, horrific acts of violence designed to tear open a gateway for even darker gods and beings to bleed through."

Sekhmet, the lion-headed goddess, stepped forward, her voice a guttural growl.

"Soon, Ammit will unleash her army upon the streets, harvesting souls for their twisted rituals. She is an abomination, and she knows it. With the Ka sword in their grasp, they could even turn their blades on the divine, sacrificing gods and goddesses to fuel their dark ambitions. And aiding them in this unholy crusade is Shezmu, the demon god of executions and slaughter."

The weight of the revelation settled on Rye's shoulders like a leaden cloak. The situation he was caught in was far more complex than he'd ever imagined. He wasn't just facing a power struggle; he was the last line of defense against a tide of unimaginable darkness.

Horus' voice crackled with urgency.

"Rye, if Set is touched by the Ka sword, he'll flee this plane. Yet, the madman craves it more than anything. Shezmu, the demon god, can be redeemed if struck by the blade and transformed from darkness to light. But be warned, he's a formidable foe."

Rye's brow furrowed.

"Death walkers?" he rasped, the term sending a shiver down his spine.

Sekhmet's response was a low rumble.

"Indeed. Nearly two thousand of them. These are soulless puppets raised by Ammit's dark magic. Unleashed upon the world, they would unleash a tide of suffering and horror. Their purpose? To herd the innocent, to fuel their masters' twisted agenda."

A steely glint hardened Rye's gaze.

"Demons hold no fear for me," he declared, his voice firm. "But we cannot allow these Death walkers to reach the people."

He envisioned these twisted creatures - stitched together fragments of death, reanimated with a single, insatiable hunger. A grotesque mockery of life, driven by a primal need to devour. This was Ammit's grand army, a blight upon the world that needed to be stopped before it could spread.

The revelation sent a jolt of purpose coursing through him. This wasn't just about regaining his freedom but safeguarding the innocent from an unimaginable evil. He was the reborn warrior, the magus, and the dance he was caught in just took a horrifying turn. But Rye, fueled by newfound power and an unyielding resolve, wouldn't back down.

Rye shuddered at the description of the Death walkers. A single one was a nightmare, but two thousand? The image of gnashing teeth, razor-sharp claws, and a relentless hunger clawed at his mind. These weren't mindless beasts; they were instruments of terror designed to inflict maximum carnage.

"We need a haven," he declared, his voice ringing with newfound resolve. "A place to gather our allies, a sanctuary where they can prepare for the coming battle in their way."

A plan began to form in his mind - a desperate gamble against overwhelming odds.

"And I'll reach out to the Zetas," he added, the name leaving his lips with a hint of hope.

The Zetas were a mysterious group rumored to possess knowledge beyond the mortal realm. They were probably their only chance.

Suddenly, a warm presence filled the chamber. Thoth, the ibis-headed god of wisdom and scribe of the gods, materialized beside him.

"Hello, Rye," his voice boomed, a symphony of knowledge and kindness. "What a glorious sight! It's a homecoming we've all been waiting for, my dear friend."

A wave of relief washed over Rye. He wasn't alone. Even in the face of such darkness, there were allies, beings of light who stood ready to fight.

"There are others like me?" he rasped, his voice thick with emotion. "Light vampires in the city?"

Thoth chuckled, a sound like wind chimes dancing in a gentle breeze.

"Indeed. A small band, but resolute. We've kept the shadows at bay for as long as possible. But Ammit and Set… their choices were made eons ago, and the dance continues. Now, a new step begins - a waltz of light against darkness. Are you ready, Rye?"

The weight of responsibility settled on Rye's shoulders, but beneath it burned a fire of purpose and determination. He wouldn't let the darkness win. He wouldn't let the innocent suffer.

"I was born ready," Rye declared, his voice ringing with newfound power.

The dance had taken a terrifying turn, but he wouldn't be a mere spectator. He was the magus, the warrior reborn, and he would fight for the light until his very last breath.

Thoth's voice grew grave.

"Unfortunately, Ammit has developed a taste for Starseeds. We know your allies are worried, and reconnecting with them is paramount."

A new figure materialized – Ma'at, the embodiment of balance and one of the Overseers who judged the affairs of gods and mortals. Her voice, a celestial chime, washed over Rye.

"True transmutation for Ammit is not merely possible, but necessary. You must send her to the Earth's core. There, she will be transformed in the planet's heart, her essence cleansed, and her sanity restored."

Rye's mind reeled.

'How could such a feat be achieved? Sending a monstrous goddess to the planet's core?'

It seemed like an impossible task.

As if sensing his doubt, Horus boomed, "We see your hesitation. But fear not. We shall guide you. Go ahead, pick up those leaves on the ground."

Rye's gaze fell upon two large leaves, seemingly ordinary, lying near his feet. A flicker of uncertainty crossed his features, but his trust in his celestial guides held firm. He bent down and retrieved them.

"Now, eat them," Horus instructed.

Rye opened his mouth, the taste of the leaves surprisingly pleasant. A surge of power coursed through him, electrifying his very being.

"You now possess nature's fire within you," Horus declared. "Flames hold no dominion over you."

Understanding dawned on Rye. This was the first step, the first weapon in his arsenal against the coming darkness. He wasn't just reborn; he was reforged, a warrior imbued with the power of nature itself. The dance had become a war, and Rye, the magus, was ready to fight.

A surge of raw power coursed through Rye. He channeled his energy, his inner essence, focusing through his eyes. With a grunt of concentration, two blazing beams of fire erupted from his sockets, igniting the concrete blocks of the museum wall like butter.

"Now, extend your arms," Horus instructed, his voice firm yet encouraging.

Obeying, Rye thrust his palms toward the roaring inferno. The flames, defying physics, twisted and writhed, tunneling into his waiting hands. He could feel the raw power crackling in his arms, thrumming through his head. His serpents, those commanding spirit guides, pulsed with satisfaction within him.

"This fire isn't just for destruction," Sekhmet interjected, her voice a rumbling caress. "It can also mend."

She materialized beside him, a vision of fierce beauty and raw power. With a flick of her wrist, she produced a pouch brimming with coins and bills.

"You'll need these," she said, handing the pouch to him.

"And pants," she added, a hint of amusement in her voice. "Form some under your thawb to hold your newfound wealth."

Ma'at, the embodiment of balance, spoke next.

"Your meeting with Ammit is two days hence, at midnight. The venue: Taposiris Magna, ruins at the city's southeastern outskirts. There, you shall encounter not just Ammit but perhaps the Ennead. Be wary, Rye. Deceptions, bargains, and hidden agendas will abound. You tread a perilous path, but you do not walk it alone. Remember that."

The weight of the revelation settled upon Rye's shoulders. A meeting with the entities behind the cosmic dance and Ammit, the fallen goddess, awaits him. The challenge was daunting, but a literal and metaphorical fire now burned within him. He was no longer the solitary vampire imprisoned in darkness.

He was the reborn magus, a warrior ignited by the power of the divine. And the dance, once a haunting melody, had morphed into a war cry, a battle for the very fate of the world. Rye, eyes blazing with newfound purpose, was ready to answer the call.

Rye straightened his back, a newfound resolve hardening his features.

"Yes, I understand," he declared, his voice ringing with quiet determination. "I'll be ready."

A flicker of curiosity crossed his expression.

"Are Ena and Mal close by?" he inquired, a sliver of hope blossoming in his chest.

The room shimmered with warmth as the gods and goddesses smiled in unison.

"They are nearby," Thoth boomed, his voice resonating with reassurance. "Your companions have held onto hope, unwavering in their faith that you would one day return."

Osiris stepped forward, his voice a deep rumble that echoed through the chamber.

"We will leave you with this knowledge, Rye. You possess everything you need to complete your mission. We will guide you, our presence a constant hum in the background, but ultimately, this is your walk. It is the challenge you set in motion eons ago, and you must see it through. Though we depart now, know that we are not truly gone. Call upon us, and we will answer."

A wave of peace washed over Rye as he bowed deeply to the celestial beings. A sense of wholeness, of activation, pulsed through him. He was no longer a fragmented spirit but a complete entity, brimming with energy and life. The world around him shimmered with a renewed clarity. His senses heightened beyond anything he'd ever known.

Intriguingly, he felt no malice toward Ammit. Instead, a strange curiosity bubbled within him.

'What awaits me at Taposiris Magna? What role am I destined to play in this cosmic dance turned war?'

"I'm most grateful," he said, his voice filled with genuine sincerity. "Thank you for your guidance and unwavering support."

He stood alone once more, yet he wasn't alone. He carried within him the power of the divine, his past legacy, and his companions' unwavering hope. The path ahead was fraught with danger, but Rye, the reborn magus, was ready.

He would face Ammit, confront the Ennead, and fight for the balance of light and darkness.

The dance had reached its crescendo, and Rye was ready to take center stage.

Chapter 3

The rising sun wasn't just a source of warmth and light; it pulsed with a strange energy, a hidden connection. It felt like a gateway: a shimmering bridge linking him to others who shared his essence, a vast network stretching across the physical world and into the boundless cosmos. Awe washed over him at the profound interconnectedness of it all.

He flexed his arm, marveling once more at the solidity of his form. The transformation had been astonishingly swift. Just hours ago, he was a fragmented spirit, a wisp of consciousness yearning for existence. Now, he stood there, a complete being, his body brimming with a vitality that bordered on the miraculous. It was a complete recovery, a complete restoration that felt like a rebirth.

Sharp and sudden, a memory pierced through the haze of his awakening. Sekhmet, the lion-headed goddess, was radiant and powerful. He recalled the weight of her presence, the reverence with which she was spoken of. And then, a curious detail – Sekhmet birthing nine vampires. It was a fragment, an enigmatic piece of a larger puzzle.

'Nine.'

The number echoed in his mind. Sekhmet birthed nine vampires on a single day, the day she supposedly became an aspect of Hathor, the goddess of joy and love. The connection seemed illogical, almost paradoxical. Three and three made six, and three was nine – a cryptic equation that sent a shiver down his spine.

It hinted at a deeper meaning, a hidden bond between these first vampires, a connection that transcended mere creation.

New questions arose.

'Were these original nine somehow linked? Did they share a special affinity, a closeness that transcended blood ties?'

The answer remained shrouded in mystery, but the seed of curiosity was firmly planted. As Rye pondered this revelation, the weight of his mission settled upon him. He wasn't just a reborn warrior but a part of something far grander, a mixture of ancient secrets and forgotten pacts.

Rye, a name that whispered of lush meadows and powerful monarchs, wasn't just reborn; he was reconnected. The memories of his companions flooded back – Mal, the name echoing with celestial purpose, a constant reminder of his angelic abilities. And Ena, her very essence radiating the serenity and harmony they all craved.

Together, they formed a pod, a haven of shared experiences and burgeoning powers. Flight, the most exhilarating of them all, became their common language. Soaring through the boundless sky, they were untouchable, a trio laughing in the face of gravity.

Yet, their journey wasn't all sunshine and soaring.

Trials by fire, they called them – battles against the dark arts, monstrous lizardmen with razor-sharp claws, and even vampires who had succumbed to the shadows.

But the darkness only fueled their euphoria. For hundreds of years, they reveled in the freedom of their existence. They explored the world like children in a boundless playground – discovering hidden waterfalls that cascaded into emerald pools, arcane caves whispering secrets of forgotten eras, and the awe-inspiring pyramids that dominated the landscape.

These weren't just magnificent structures; they were generators, activators, humming with a power they yearned to understand. They spent ages within these pyramids, unraveling their mysteries and activating dormant mechanisms. But even in their moments of greatest triumph, the dance with darkness lurked at the edges.

It was a constant reminder that their existence was not without its perils. The shadows never truly slept, and Rye, Mal, and Ena knew, with unshakeable certainty, that one day, they would have to face the darkness head-on.

One harrowing encounter forever etched itself into their memories. It was an ambush – dark lizardmen, reptilian brutes with eyes like molten lava, launched a surprise attack. The first weapon they wielded wasn't fangs or claws but a horrifying assault on their very minds.

Their telepathic connection, the silent language binding them, was scrambled into a chaotic mess. Images blinked before their eyes – a horrifying kaleidoscope of torture, limbs severed, bodies mutilated, their souls shattered. It was a deliberate attempt to sow confusion and terror, to break their bond and exploit their vulnerability.

Fear threatened to consume them. But Rye, ever the protector, held firm. He bore the brunt of the psychic assault, a nightmare blade carving invisible wounds in his spirit. The pain was excruciating, a chilling premonition of what awaited them if they faltered. Just as despair threatened to engulf him, a blinding light erupted from within.

An ancient presence, a being they knew only as Stanne, surged forward, a benevolent spirit answering their unspoken plea. With a gesture of immense power, Stanne channeled the collective strength of unseen entities, a multitude of guardian hands reaching forth to shield Rye from the onslaught.

The reptilian attackers recoiled, their assault broken. The psychic assault subsided, leaving behind a chilling silence. Rye clung to his newfound awareness, weak but alive – they weren't alone. In the face of darkness, a beacon of light had emerged, a protector who watched over them from the unseen realms.

This encounter prompted the true cost of their existence. The dance with darkness was no mere metaphor; it was a constant battle, a war waged not just on the physical plane but within their minds.

The reptilian attackers, driven by a monstrous hunger for chaos and control, were a stark reminder of the true enemy.

Their sole purpose was domination, their weapons fear and the insidious whispers of madness. Countless noble souls had succumbed to their mind-numbing tactics, their spirits broken, their wills shattered.

Rye, marked by the psychic scars of the battle, now walked a precarious tightrope, forever a hair's breadth from the abyss. The nightmare blade had inflicted a deep wound, a chilling reminder of his vulnerability. Yet, amidst the darkness, a beacon of hope emerged.

Enter the Starseeds. These aren't mere mortals but celestial beings, star-stuff brought into human form. Possessing the combined wisdom and power of their elders, they intervened at the critical juncture. With a coordinated effort, they severed the very fabric of the reptilian's psychic assault, slamming the portal shut before it could fully engulf Rye.

These monstrous lizardmen, for now, were thwarted. Their attempts to exploit his weakened state had been met with an unshakeable defense.

Rye exerted a sigh of relief. He squeezed his eyes shut, the memory of those unseen guardians, the Starseeds, a comforting weight in his mind. A wry smile touched his lips.

'*Yes,*' he thought, a newfound determination hardening his resolve. *'There are far more pleasant things to contemplate than reptilian scum.'*

The memory of their shared adventures, the exhilarating freedom of flight, the awe-inspiring secrets they had unraveled – these were the things that truly mattered. The darkness would always be there, a lurking threat at the edges of their existence. But now, Rye knew he wasn't alone. He had celestial and earthly allies, and together, they would face whatever horrors awaited them.

As Rye contemplated the nature of his Star Being allies, a sense of wonder washed over him. These celestial beings weren't just powerful entities; they were a reflection, in some ways, of the gods he'd just encountered.

Unlike the distant, mythologized figures of legend, the Star Beings actively participated in the cosmic drama. They hailed from a dazzling array of star systems, some perhaps even within our own Milky Way galaxy, their forms a testament to the vast diversity of the cosmos.

However, unlike the power-hungry deities of human lore, the Star Beings weren't driven by conquest or dominion. Their purpose was far nobler – to act as guides, nudging humanity and its supernatural counterparts toward a brighter future. Their presence wasn't a flashy intervention; it was a subtle influence, a guiding hand on the shoulder of existence.

Their ability to blend in was uncanny. They could seamlessly integrate into human society, their true nature masked from casual observation. They were masters of disguise, able to walk among mortals as ordinary people.

Yet, when the situation demanded, they could vanish into a higher plane of existence, becoming invisible to the naked eye. This ability to shift realities spoke volumes about their profound connection to a higher order, a dimension beyond the physical world's limitations.

Though seemingly improbable at first glance, this alliance with the Star Beings held a deeper logic when viewed through the lens of their lifespans. With their extended existence, Vampires and Star Beings, with their potentially infinite lifespans, possessed a vast perspective on the grand cosmic dance. They understood the importance of balance, the delicate equilibrium between light and darkness.

Their goals were fundamentally aligned – to ensure harmony prevailed over chaos. This shared purpose and commitment to the greater good destined their paths to converge across the vastness of space and time.

These Star Beings weren't just powerful allies but companions bound by millennia of shared purpose. They were the unseen guardians, the celestial siblings who walked alongside the "eternal living," those like Rye who defied the boundaries of mortality.

Together, they strived toward the highest good, a silent force for balance in a universe teetering on the edge. He wasn't a solitary warrior facing an insurmountable challenge; he was part of a cosmic family. The weight of his mission, though daunting, felt lighter now. He wasn't alone in this dance; he had a legion of celestial siblings by his side, ready to face the shadows and fight for the very fate of the world.

A glimmer of recognition sparked in Rye's eyes as he absorbed the details about the Star Beings. So, they weren't a monolithic entity but a diverse collective! Names like Sirians and Pleiadians danced in his mind, each whispering of a different origin story, a unique set of abilities.

The Sirians, beings from the constellation Canis Major, resonated with a particular warmth. Their reputation for benevolence and innovation mirrored the enigmatic figures who had guided him within the pyramids.

'Could it be that these Star Beings, with their advanced technology, were the ones who had assisted the ancient Egyptians in their monumental constructions?'

The thought sent a shiver down his spine. Perhaps those weren't just pyramids; they were gateways, conduits that facilitated communication with beings from beyond the stars.

Then there were the Pleiadians, the near-albino humanoids from the Pleiades star system. Their mission of fostering world peace and guiding humanity away from self-destruction resonated deeply with Rye. He understood, now more than ever, the precarious state of the world, the delicate balance between harmony and chaos.

'Perhaps the Starseeds, those humans imbued with Pleiadian essence, were the quiet heroes working from within.'

The revelation sparked a multitude of questions within him.

The answers remained elusive, but the knowledge itself was empowering. He wasn't just a pawn in a cosmic game but part of a grand design, a network of light across the galaxy.

The Sirians, with their transmutation abilities, and the Pleiadians, with their defense of peace, were the celestial siblings he might encounter on his journey. Each encounter held the promise of new knowledge and allies in the fight against the encroaching darkness—a newfound determination hardened in Rye's chest.

The dance had taken on a new dimension, a cosmic ballet with players from across the stars. And Rye, the warrior reborn, was somewhat able to perform to his fullest.

As the sun dipped below the horizon, painting the sky in a mesmerizing blend of oranges, pinks, and yellows, Rye couldn't help but be awestruck.

'Amazing,' he thought, a dry smile playing on his lips. *'This is the most active day I've had in five hundred years.'*

The bustling city stretched before him, starkly contrasting the stillness of his imprisonment. Towering buildings, their facades reflecting the fading light, lined the curving streets. Glowing signs cast an electric buzz, a stark contrast to the oil lamps of his past life. It was both familiar and strangely alien, a testament to the passage of time.

Yet, the element that truly captivated him was the constant hum of automobiles. In all shapes and sizes, these metal beasts zipped through the concrete jungle, their flashing lights and honking horns creating a symphony of chaos. It was a far cry from the horse-drawn carriages of his memories, but Rye found himself strangely enthralled by their speed and maneuverability. To him, the congested streets resembled a battlefield, each driver a warrior vying for position.

A mischievous glint sparked in his eyes.

'Tomorrow,' he thought, indulging his newfound curiosity. *'I might just borrow one of these "vehicles" to explore the marketplace.'*

After all, he only had two days before his fateful meeting with Ammit.

He truly had no idea what to expect, what horrors this twisted goddess might unleash.

But amidst the suspense, a flash of determination ignited within him. He wouldn't go into this blind. He would spend the remaining hours learning, gathering intel, and preparing for whatever challenges awaited him. He was Rye, the reborn warrior, and he wouldn't face the shadows alone. He had his celestial allies, the Sirians, the Pleiadians, and perhaps even the enigmatic Arcturians, rumored to be the most advanced beings in the galaxy.

With renewed resolve, Rye adjusted his position, his gaze fixed on the glittering cityscape. The dance was far from over, but he was ready to take the next step. The fate of the world, perhaps even the galaxy, hung in the balance, and Rye, the warrior reborn, was prepared for full participation.

Chapter 4

Darkness was draped over the city like a cloak, transforming the beautiful sprawl into a mesmerizing allure of twinkling lights. A restless energy pulsed through Rye. Once a tolerable perch, the museum wall now felt like a cage. He yearned for a change of scenery, to witness the bustling city metamorphose under the cloak of night.

With a silent decision, he stretched, his muscles pleasantly surprised by their disuse after centuries of slumber. He turned to head back inside, amusement flickering across his mind. Just moments ago, he'd been enthralled by the marvels of modern technology – towering structures scraping the sky, metal beasts zipping through the concrete jungle.

Now, a more immediate concern surfaced – how would he slip back into the museum unseen?

Laced with the rediscovery of a forgotten ability, a grin stretched across his face. With a focused thought, he phased through the seemingly solid seam of the doorway. The physical world offered no resistance as he passed through the barrier. Back within the dimly lit museum, his eyes were immediately drawn to the fossilized snake head, its intricate carvings and petrified form a contrast to the sleek modernity he'd just witnessed.

An inexplicable pull resonated from the relic. He reached out, and his touch was reverent as he cradled the cool stone in his hands.

"Quite a day, wouldn't you say?" he murmured, a hint of surprise filled his voice.

Silence stretched for a beat, and then, to his utter astonishment, a voice rasped from within the fossilized skull.

"I can help you understand this new era whenever you pick me up," the snake head rasped.

Its voice was a dry whisper that echoed through the chamber. Rye's eyes widened. This was unlike anything he'd encountered before.

A talking relic, a bridge between the ancient past and the perplexing present? The revelation sent excitement through him. Perhaps, just perhaps, this fossilized serpent held the key to unlocking the mysteries of his new reality.

"Cameras," Serpent grated. "The archive and the museum exterior are crawling with them."

Relief flooded Rye. Despite the cameras, the serpent assured him of his unique state of being, and conjured clothes rendered him invisible.

"There are two more down here, tucked away," the serpent rasped, indicating diagonal corners.

"Thank you," Rye said with genuine appreciation. "Those cameras... completely slipped my mind. These new tools and machines will take some learning."

The serpent chuckled dryly.

"Of course. Imagine the jumbled state of your mind after so long."

Restless energy crackled in Rye's eyes.

"Exactly. I need to stretch my legs and be done with this sarcophagus."

He glanced at it with disdain.

"I'd love to summon Isis and Thoth and see if we can deal with this… tub. I wouldn't mind crushing it."

He paused, hope flickering in his gaze before he continued, "More importantly, I need Isis' guidance on finding lodging."

Thoth and Isis materialized within the archive, their forms solidifying from shimmering motes of light.

"This might be our farewell to the archive," Rye remarked, a touch of sadness in his voice. "A challenging experience, one etched in my memory."

Rye's gaze snagged on the sarcophagus, and a knot of dread tightened in his gut. It wasn't just a stone coffin anymore; it was a physical manifestation of his torment – the isolation, the bone-chilling cold, the sheer terror of being trapped for centuries.

He scanned its surface, searching for meaning in the stark emptiness – no hieroglyphs, symbols, nothing to offer solace or explanation. It was a crude cement tub, the lid resting askew, a grim reminder of his forced slumber.

Memories flooded back, sharp and brutal. Set, the embodiment of chaos, had driven a needle, laced with enough poison to fell a god, deep into his leg. Then came Ammit, the devourer of souls, shoving him into this tomb with a final, cruel shove.

But it wasn't just her doing.

A cold understanding settled over him.

'This was Set's plan, and Ammit, in a twisted turn, had become his accomplice. She combined her wicked curse, a legacy of darkness passed down through generations, with Set's malevolent power, binding me to this prison. This,' he realized, his jaw clenching. *'Is the genesis of their unholy alliance.'*

Isis' voice, however, cut through the tension.

"There are several good hotels just half an hour from here," she said. "I know a nice one with plenty of space for both you and your allies. It could even serve as a command center of sorts. I'll take care of making the arrangements."

"Thank you so much," Rye replied. "I'm still getting used to how things are around here."

"Perfectly understandable," Isis replied with a gentle smile.

Thoth boomed, his voice resonating with authority.

"Now, about this sarcophagus."

He materialized a thick glass cube, surprisingly small considering the sarcophagus' size and cradled it in his feathered palm. He muttered an incantation with his other hand outstretched toward the stone coffin. The sarcophagus shimmered and shrunk, condensing until it fit neatly within the confines of the cube. Thoth tucked the cube securely beneath his chest feathers.

"I'll ensure its safekeeping," he declared.

"Thank you, my friend," Rye said with a sigh of relief. "Good riddance to that thing for a while."

As they waited for Isis to finalize the hotel arrangements, Rye slipped outside, eager to stretch his legs and experience the night air. The dry breeze carried the scent of the city, a stark contrast to the stale air of the museum archive. As he stood there, taking it all in, Thoth and Isis materialized beside him.

"Your snake head, sir," Isis said with a knowing smile, handing him the fossilized relic. "The hotel is all set. You have the top suite, which is complimentary for a month. After that, we'll figure something out."

"My deepest gratitude, my guide," Rye replied, a genuine smile on his face.

"You know," he began hesitantly. "I could use some company. A walk with friends, not just me alone."

He looked hopefully at Isis and Thoth.

"Perhaps a stroll to the hotel?" he suggested.

A chorus of agreement echoed in the night air.

"Certainly," boomed Thoth, while Isis simply smiled and nodded.

"Definitely," she added.

Together, the unlikely trio set off, Rye, the warrior reborn, venturing into the neon-lit cityscape with his celestial allies.

Isis' voice whispered in his ear, the sound calming and informative.

"Thoth and I will accompany you. We'll be invisible to the human eye and ear, but you'll see us as usual. Take your time, Rye. Savor this walk. People will only be able to perceive you."

Dusk had descended. The sun dipped below the horizon, casting an ethereal glow on the metropolis. The last rays of sunlight danced across the buildings, highlighting their glass and steel surfaces.

Rye clutched the fossilized snake head, its coolness a grounding presence in his hand. With Isis and Thoth by his invisible side, he set off. His footsteps echoed softly against the pavement, the only sound breaking the gentle hum of the city's nighttime pulse.

They turned the corner, and the museum's imposing facade rose. Floodlights bathed the building in a warm, golden light, revealing intricate carvings and architectural details that whispered of a bygone era. Rye stopped, his gaze lingering on the weathered stone. A smile touched his lips as he approached a nearby placard.

"A citadel for so long," he murmured, reading the inscription aloud, the words echoing softly in the stillness of the night.

Thoth stepped forward, a curious object materializing in his hand. It resembled a circle with a perpendicular bar extending from one side, broader than a man's shoulders – the top portion of an Ankh.

"Here," he rumbled, his voice resonating with power. "Allow me to offer you this."

The object pulsed with a faint light as Thoth explained its purpose.

"I can program this key, granting you mastery of over twenty languages. It will account for how languages like Arabic and English have evolved over the past five centuries."

With a practiced motion, Thoth swept the Ankh over Rye's head and down to his feet, then back up, completing a symbolic circle.

"As above, so below; as below, so above."

The Ankh vanished back into Thoth's possession.

"A language upgrade," Rye breathed, feeling a wave of gratitude washing over him. "Thank you, truly."

Leaving the museum behind, they crossed a bridge walkway. The cool night air was a welcome change from the stale museum atmosphere. It invigorated Rye, a fresh energy coursing through him.

"My legs," he whispered, the sensation of movement after centuries a foreign yet exhilarating feeling.

The night thrummed with activity; people strolled along the bridge, their faces bathed in the warm glow of streetlamps. A genuine smile stretched across Rye's face.

The world around him was a fusion of sights and sounds. Every detail – the colors, the intricate patterns on clothing, the way leaves rustled on nearby trees – seemed amplified, imbued with a life he hadn't noticed before. He flexed his leg muscles, marveling at the network of sinew and bone beneath his skin. He felt raw, stripped bare of anything extraneous, a being of pure sensation.

"I haven't seen my reflection yet," he said to his unseen companions, a flicker of curiosity sparking in his eyes.

They continued their walk, following the sidewalk that curved northward along the darkening Mediterranean. The once-blue water had taken on an indigo hue, reflecting the deepening twilight.

Rye stopped, captivated by the sight. These waters held a special significance for him, a portal to his past. Here, he was a man out of time, a fragment of the ancient world thrust into the modern one, surrounded by echoes of a bygone era.

A movement on the water's surface caught his eye. He squinted, trying to discern his reflection. It wasn't a clear image, but it was enough. He could see the length of his black hair, past his ears, hair he could pull back if he chose. A tanned face stared back, with a strong jaw and cheekbones.

A pang of longing pierced him. He missed her. The keeper of his Lemurian seed crystal - a woman who would have understood and who would have been here beside him. But now, not even a phantom remained.

She was gone, vanished without a trace.

The thought of following her path flickered across his mind, a chilling possibility. Yet, he pushed it down. There was too much to learn and experience in this new world.

'This is why I stayed,' he reminded himself.

The weight of his past momentarily forgotten, he turned his attention to the present. The darkness, he knew, was already stirring, its agents plotting their next move.

"To fly again," he uttered with a yearning echo.

"Ah, yes, to fly again," Isis responded, her voice a comforting whisper in his ear. "Let's not delay."

Following her instruction, Rye stepped up as if onto the first step of an invisible staircase. A jolt of energy surged through him, lifting him two feet off the ground.

"I remember!" he exclaimed, a thrill coursing through him. "As long as I can get that initial lift, the rest comes naturally."

"Exactly," Isis confirmed.

Rye focused, picturing the soles of his feet. He pushed down, willing himself upwards. And up he went, soaring past startled birds and tree branches, the cool night air whipping through his hair. He was free! He climbed higher, reveling in the exhilaration of flight, his playground's vast expanse of the night sky. He swooped and soared, a warrior reborn, embracing the freedom he had yearned for for centuries.

Three bursts of speed, a quick dash forward and back, then another, and another. With each surge, Rye launched himself higher, arms outstretched for balance. Up, up he went, the earth's curvature gradually revealing itself beneath him. The city lights twinkled like scattered jewels, a testament to human ingenuity. At this altitude, the vast deserts stretched like silent chronicles of time, their stillness whispering ancient secrets.

He became dizzy.

He knew it was time to descend. But Rye indulged in a slow, 360-degree spin, savoring the breathtaking panorama before he did. The world stretched out beneath him, a vibrant tapestry of light and darkness.

With a gentle nudge of his will, Rye began his descent. The air thickened around him, the sensation of breathing becoming easier. He hovered for a moment just above the treetops, basking in the afterglow of the flight.

'It's stunning,' he thought.

"Isn't it?" Isis whispered in his ear, a touch of amusement lacing her words. "The freedom of flight. A gift of the heavens."

"Unmatched," Rye replied, his voice filled with awe. "It does something profound to the soul."

"And the mind," Isis added softly. "And the heart."

Ignoring the urge to dwell on historical details, Rye refocused on the present. He, Isis, and Thoth continued their walk along the curving path that hugged the Mediterranean coastline. The once-bustling sidewalk had thinned as the night deepened. Street lamps cast long shadows, painting the walkway in a mosaic of light and darkness.

Signs and road directions confirmed what Rye already knew – Alexandria remained under Muslim rule. A flicker of recognition crossed his face. It had been the same during his previous life, a golden age etched in his memory. A hearty laugh escaped his lips as a stream of cars whizzed, starkly contrasting the horse-drawn carriages of his bygone era.

The cityscape transformed as they neared the hotel. The throngs of people thinned, replaced by a more peaceful tranquility. Here, the whisper of the waves against the shore became the dominant sound.

Isis materialized a sleek passport in her hand, a mischievous smile playing on her lips.

"Your name at the hotel, Rye Jalal," she announced. "And here's your passport. As legit as a thousand-year-old vampire can be, that is."

Rye took the passport, his fingers tracing the embossed lettering. He flipped it open, his breath catching in his throat. A stranger stared back at him from the photo – a handsome man with dark hair and piercing eyes. A flicker of uncertainty crossed his face.

"Is that… me?" he asked, his voice barely a whisper.

"Indeed it is," Thoth boomed, a hint of amusement in his voice. "A manifestation of your current form."

"I don't need to ask how easy it is for you to do that," Rye chuckled, a nervous edge to his laughter. "But now I have a real idea of my appearance."

Thoth dipped his head in a shallow nod.

"Even for some advanced vampires, manifesting physical form is limited. Light vampires, for instance, can only conjure clothing, while some can manifest weapons. It's a balancing act, accepting your limitations."

Rye agreed.

"However," Thoth continued, his voice resonating with authority. "The clothes you conjure are an extension of yourself. Only you can remove them, and they are nearly indestructible."

They reached the hotel, a beacon of warm light against the night sky. Rye glanced around, a sense of apprehension battling with excitement. The lobby was a tasteful blend of modern luxury and timeless elegance. Soft lighting bathed the space warmly, casting inviting shadows around plush armchairs and deep mahogany tables.

Gilded accents framed rich burgundy drapes, and the thick red carpet cushioned his footsteps. The air held a subtle scent of incense, not overpowering but pleasant. A sense of spaciousness and a deliberate lack of clutter allowed the eye to rest. It was a world away from his spartan tomb, yet somehow… comforting.

With a deep breath, Rye squared his shoulders and approached the front desk. He stood there for a moment, gathering his courage.

"Good evening," he began, his voice slightly hoarse from disuse. "I believe I have a reservation under the name Rye Jalal?"

He slid the passport across the counter, his gaze flickering between the polished marble surface and the immaculately dressed clerk behind it.

"Ah, yes sir, welcome," the receptionist greeted warmly, a genuine smile spreading across his face. "We've been expecting you. Thank you for your identification."

Rye watched as the man, Ibrahim by his nametag, flipped through the passport with practiced ease. A moment later, a packet materialized in his hand.

"Here you have it, Mr. Jalal," he explained, placing it on the counter. "Your key cards, a full menu for your convenience, pamphlets with local activities, and all our contact information. We want to ensure you have a comfortable stay."

Relief washed over Rye as he accepted the packet.

"Thank you very much," he said, his voice finding strength. "I appreciate it. And what might your name be?"

"Ibrahim, at your service, Mr. Jalal. A pleasure to meet you. We received your friends earlier this evening. They brought up your luggage and belongings."

Surprise crossed Rye's face but was quickly replaced by a smile.

"Excellent," he said.

"Sounds like things are moving smoothly."

"Indeed, sir," Ibrahim confirmed, glancing at the clock on the wall. "Almost nine ten."

"Perfect," Rye replied, tucking the packet securely under his arm. "Thank you again."

"You're quite welcome, sir. And don't hesitate to call if you need anything. Our main desk number is right here, as is the bar service, which runs until two in the morning."

With a final nod of appreciation, Rye turned away from the counter. The grand staircase, carpeted in a plush burgundy with white accents, beckoned him upwards. He climbed with a newfound lightness in his step, the thick banister cool beneath his fingers. Reaching the landing, he turned left, continuing his ascent to the second and third floors before finally arriving at his destination – the fifth floor.

He momentarily fumbled with the key card, a small tremor of uncertainty running through him. A soft click confirmed success, and the door swung open, revealing a sight that stole his breath away.

"We made it, Isis and Thoth," he whispered, stepping inside. "What a beautiful room!"

Rye wandered through the suite, overwhelmed by the sheer abundance. Each room held its allure – the plush comfort of the bedroom, the sleek kitchen functionality, the quiet promise of knowledge in the study. But the living area, bathed in the soft glow of strategically placed lamps, drew him in.

He sank onto a plush sofa, the coolness of the leather a welcome contrast to the warmth of his body. The weight of the past centuries pressed down on him, a heavy cloak.

"Sleep," Thoth had said.

But sleep, for Rye, was a treacherous terrain filled with fragmented memories and haunting nightmares.

His gaze drifted to the stack of DVDs. Movies. A sliver of curiosity sparked within him.

'What were these "plays" of the modern world like?'

He picked one up, feeling the cool plastic in his hand. A fantastical image adorned the cover – a group of strange creatures battling fantastical beasts. It was…intriguing.

With a sigh, Rye rose and walked over to the large window that dominated one wall of the room. Alexandria stretched out before him. Nostalgia washed over him. He could almost hear the bustling marketplace and smell the fragrant spices that filled the air.

A soft voice startled him.

"The city hasn't changed much, has it?"

Isis materialized beside him, her form shimmering like moonlight on water.

Rye shook his head, a bittersweet smile tugging at his lips.

"The buildings are different, taller. But the soul of the city… that remains the same."

They stood in companionable silence for a long while, lost in their thoughts. Finally, Isis turned to him, her eyes filled with concern.

"You haven't forgotten why we're here, have you, Rye?"

He met her gaze, his expression resolute.

"Never. But tonight…tonight, I think I just need a moment to breathe. To remember who I was before I became this."

He gestured vaguely at himself.

Isis nodded, understanding flickering in her ancient eyes.

"Take your time, friend. We won't rush you."

With a grateful glance, Rye turned back to the window. The cityscape beckoned, a siren song of the familiar and the unknown. A decision flickered in his mind.

'Perhaps a walk through the streets and a chance to reconnect with the city of my past are exactly what I need.'

Chapter 5

As night reluctantly surrendered to dawn, Rye was drawn to the rooftop. The first blush of sunrise peeked over the eastern horizon, painting the sky in soft hues of pink and orange. The city below, still shrouded in the remnants of darkness, slowly began to stir. Once mere silhouettes, buildings emerged from the shadows, their windows catching the first golden rays of light.

Rye had spent the night wide awake. A restless energy was coursing through him. He'd attempted to watch a movie, the novelty of the format initially captivating. But the flickering images on the screen couldn't hold his attention. Yesterday's whirlwind of emotions – the shock of awakening, the overwhelming bounty in his suite – all demanded a quieter space for reflection. However, venturing outside at 3 a.m. seemed unwise, so he sought solace on the rooftop.

Here, situated in a secluded corner, a flat expanse of rooftops offered a perfect vantage point. Rye stretched out on his back. The cool stone beneath him was a welcome contrast to the warmth radiating from his body. Above him, a breathtaking canvas unfolded – a vast expanse of night sky studded with a dazzling array of stars. The city lights, twinkling like scattered diamonds, gradually dimmed as the first rays of dawn painted the eastern sky.

As the sun ascended, bathing the city in its golden light, a sense of purpose settled over Rye. He had a plan. Tomorrow, he would visit the bustling marketplace, which held cherished memories from his previous life. He needed to reconnect with the city's pulse and immerse himself in the sights and sounds so deeply attached to his being. He yearned for the bartering merchants, the intoxicating aroma of exotic spices, and the colors that filled the market stalls. It was a piece of his past he desperately craved.

The meeting with Ammit loomed large, a shadow at the edge of his consciousness. But for now, he would focus on the present, on reclaiming a part of himself that had been lost for centuries. With a deep breath, Rye rose from his rooftop sanctuary, the rising sun a beacon guiding him toward a new day.

The rooftop offered a panoramic view of the city and a glimpse of the vast Mediterranean Sea. The first rays of dawn danced on its surface, setting the water ablaze with a thousand sparkling diamonds. The sight triggered a potent wave of nostalgia, transporting Rye back to a time before the suffocating darkness of the sarcophagus. He could almost taste the salty spray on his lips and feel the warm sun on his skin. But the idyllic memories were fleeting, chased away by the unwelcome specters that haunted his dreams – the cold, dank confines of his tomb.

For now, however, he chose to focus on the present. This morning, he had accepted a new identity. Gone were the tattered remnants of his past life; in their place, a simple yet elegant tan thawb, its color reminiscent of the desert sands. He had swept his hair back, revealing a face that, despite its ageless quality, held the promise of a fresh start.

A tantalizing aroma wafted up from below, a symphony of sizzling meats and frying eggs. It was the city waking up, the smell of breakfast mingling with the salty tang of the sea breeze. A cheerful chirp broke the silence – a small bird, perched on the rooftop's edge, had come to greet the day alongside Rye.

A sense of optimism bloomed in his chest. It was going to be a good day. A taxi ride to the bustling marketplace awaited a place where he could indulge in the modern marvel of a wristwatch – a practical and stylish accessory. A map, too, was essential, a key to unlocking the secrets of this new and ever-evolving city. Beyond that, he simply wanted to wander, lose himself in human life, and savor the sights, sounds, and smells of a reborn world.

"That sounds good."

A soft murmur startled Rye from his contemplation. Isis materialized beside him. The sheer brilliance of her form was almost overwhelming, forcing him to avert his gaze momentarily.

"Thanks," Rye replied, his voice tinged with a newfound hope. "There's so much to catch up on, so many people to see again. How much has the city grown?"

Isis settled beside him, her voice a soothing melody.

"Over five and a half million people call Alexandria home now."

"I need a world map, too," Rye continued, a spark of determination lighting his eyes. "There's so much to learn, so much that's changed."

A shadow of understanding whispered across Isis' face.

"Be patient with yourself, Rye," she said gently. "Reclaiming your place in the world will take time. But you are strong, more resilient than you realize."

With a gesture as graceful as a desert windblown wisp, Isis reached out and cradled Rye's head. A warm energy pulsed from her, and a green glow emanated from her very core. Rye closed his eyes, surrendering to the sensation.

He felt a pure, crystalline white light descend from above, bathing his being in its brilliance. It converged with his own heart, igniting a warmth that spread through him like wildfire. It was a profound connection, a deep communion that resonated at the very core of his existence.

Isis bowed her head in silent reverence, offering a silent prayer to the unseen forces that guided them.

When she spoke again, her voice was filled with conviction.

"You are strong, Rye. Your journey and your suffering all have meaning. Answers are waiting to be discovered. Let's stand."

Rye rose to his feet, his gaze locked with Isis'. Her form shimmered with an ethereal luminescence. He closed his eyes once more, and an image flooded his mind's eye. The white light descended again but traveled a different path this time. It flowed from the heavens, engulfing him, then continued its journey down his spine, burrowing deep into the earth itself.

"Push it down, Rye," Isis instructed, her voice soft yet firm. "Push it as far as you can go. Deeper. Deeper still. Feel the earth embrace it."

Rye obeyed, but the effort was a physical and mental strain. It felt like his head was expanding, the fog of confusion and fear lifting with each surge of light. Clarity washed over him, dispelling the shadows of his long imprisonment. A surge of overwhelming emotion welled within him – a potent cocktail of gratitude, joy, and a profound sense of belonging. He yearned to share it and express the immensity of his feelings.

Isis pressed a small, ornately decorated container into Rye's hand.

"This is for you," she explained. "For your continued healing. My milk."

Rye stared at the vessel, curiosity flickering across his face.

"May I ask what it is?"

"It is mine," Isis replied, her voice resonating with a quiet power. "My milk."

There was a spark of understanding in Rye's eyes.

"We will be truly connected then," he murmured, a sense of awe washing over him.

Isis offered a reassuring smile.

"Indeed. We can count on it."

With a steady hand, Rye uncorked the container and tipped it back, the divine essence flowing smoothly down his throat. As he finished, Isis gently placed her hand over his heart, a current of warm energy pulsating from her touch.

"There is a reason I was compelled to seek you out, Rye," she said softly. "You carry a deep wound, a pain that lingers after centuries. I am here to offer solace, be your balm and healer, and guide you through the many paths to wholeness."

Rye met her gaze, captivated by the depths reflected in her golden eyes. The potent psychic energy crackling between them was an undeniable force. A sense of profound connection bloomed within him, urging him closer.

Without a word, they embraced. It was a silent communion that transcended words. Overwhelmed by the surge of emotion, Rye leaned down, his lips seeking the soft skin of her neck. Isis offered no resistance, a low moan escaping her lips as she arched closer.

Pushing against his chest, she whispered, "We will mend, Rye. Together, we will heal and love again."

Their lips met in a kiss. It was a cosmic connection, a sharing of souls as ancient as time itself. In that shared moment, Rye saw visions – the Ankh, its two serpents coiling around the base, mirroring Isis' cobra gracing the top. It was a symbol of their bond, a testament to the powerful forces at play.

Drawing back slightly, Rye gazed into her eyes.

"Ready to explore the market together?"

Isis' lips curved into a radiant smile.

"That sounds delightful. I shall inform Thoth of our whereabouts."

"Excellent," Rye said, a newfound energy coursing through him. "Then we're all set. Time to hail a taxi and lose ourselves in vibrant chaos."

***

A mischievous glint flickered in Rye's eyes as he made a decision. Rising effortlessly above the rooftop, he ascended two or three feet, a silent phantom against the backdrop of the rising sun. He drifted sideways, scanning the perimeter for any prying eyes. Satisfied with the solitude, he descended gracefully, landing silently beside Isis.

Her ochre dress, bathed in the morning light, accentuated her otherworldly beauty. Rye couldn't help but acknowledge the tug in his chest – this was going to be a challenge, a captivating dance he was determined to embrace.

"Alright, how do we hail a taxi?" Rye projected the question telepathically, their newfound mode of communication.

Isis, ever the pragmatist, offered a reassuring smile.

"Simple, Rye. Taxis typically wait at hotels for fares."

"Excellent," Rye replied. "Where are we headed?"

"Two options," Isis explained. "Zan an Al Sitat, a bustling haven for shoppers, or Khan el-Khalili Soak, Alexandria's oldest market."

He was again filled with nostalgia.

"Remarkable," he sent back telepathically. "Khan el-Khalili Soak existed even during my earlier time here. Let's head there, a walk down memory lane, would you say?"

"Sounds perfect," Isis agreed, her voice tinged with excitement.

Together, they strolled toward the hotel entrance. Eager to hail their ride, Rye walked a few steps beyond the doors, where a bright yellow taxi stood against the morning light. Its black-painted squares around the tires seemed almost playful. A lone driver leaned casually by the front fender, his posture relaxed.

"Hello," Rye greeted him with a friendly wave.

"Good morning to you too, sir!" the driver replied, his voice exclaiming with a welcoming cheer. "How can I help you today?"

"We'd like a ride to Khan el-Khalili Soak," Rye explained.

The driver's eyes gleamed with delight.

"Excellent choice! A treasure trove waiting to be explored! How does EGP40 sound? That's roughly two and a half dollars if you prefer."

A silent message flashed between Rye and Isis – a shared thought of approval.

"That's great," Isis confirmed telepathically.

"Perfect," Rye said aloud, confirming the fare.

"Let the adventure begin!" the driver declared with a flourish, his enthusiasm infectious.

Rye was thrilled with anticipation. He grasped the handle of the right rear door, a familiar action that sent him a jolt of unexpected pleasure. The door, yellow with age and adorned with its minor dents, creaked open with a sigh. He ushered Isis in first, then followed her onto the worn black bench seat. Reaching into his pouch, he fished out two crisp E£20 coins, the cool metal a tangible link to his new reality.

As Rye pressed two £20 coins into the driver's hand – one for the fare, another as a generous tip – a grin stretched across the driver's face.

"Many thanks, my friend!" he bellowed, his voice brimming with genuine appreciation. "And tell me, how long have you graced Alexandria with your presence?"

Rye chuckled, a touch hesitant.

"Oh, a fairly long time," he replied, the weight of centuries unspoken.

The driver's eyes narrowed in a playful squint.

"Your Arabic is quite fascinating," he observed. "A curious mix of old and new, almost like a melody from a bygone era."

Rye shrugged, a flicker of amusement dancing in his eyes.

"Well, I suppose that's true for most of us in one way or another, isn't it?" he said, gazing out the window at the bustling streets.

Buildings, shops, and a throng of people flowed past.

"Indeed," the driver conceded. "But there's something truly unique about your speech, a certain inflection and choice of words that makes me pause. Excellent! It will be a powerful tool for bartering in the market!"

Rye glanced out the windshield, the chaotic dance of cars and motorbikes vying for space captivating him. He used his ESP to identify a boxy taxi he himself found – a Lada, a testament to a bygone era of Soviet manufacturing.

"Are most taxis here Ladas?" he inquired, a hint of nostalgia lacing his voice. "It's been a while since I've kept track."

The driver chuckled.

"No problem, sir! This is my trusty Lada. It is a bit of a relic, but she still runs strong. Regular oil changes," he winked. "The not-so-secret secret to a long-lasting car."

"Do you own a car yourself?" he asked curiously.

Rye shook his head.

"Not at the moment," he admitted. "But it's a future consideration."

Isis, seated beside him, couldn't help but smile. With its sights, sounds, and sheer volume of life, this new world was already awakening something long dormant within Rye.

As they neared their destination, the driver announced, "We're almost there, sir! Here's wishing you the best of luck in your search."

He pulled the Lada to a stop just beyond the grand entrance of the Khan el-Khalili Soak. Rye leaned forward, offering his gratitude.

"Thank you very much, my friend. We appreciate it."

"The pleasure was all mine!" the driver said, leaning out his window. "Now, remember, keep your eyes peeled and explore every nook and cranny! You never know what treasures you might find." With a hearty laugh, he hopped back into his car and sped off.

Rye's gaze lingered on the receding Lada, then shifted toward Isis. Her ochre dress flowed gracefully around her, framed by a reddish hijab that revealed a glimpse of her jet-black hair. The Egyptian sun cast a warm glow on her face, highlighting the spark of excitement in her eyes.

"Shall we begin?" she asked.

A smile lit on Rye's face.

"Yes," he replied. "Let's explore the wonders that await us."

Chapter 6

Stepping through the threshold, Khan el-Khalili unfolded before Rye like a meticulously preserved jewel box. The air was warm, filled with a honeyed glow from overhead lamps, casting a golden patina over this world of commerce. Arched walkways, bristling with merchants' displays, formed a tunnel, a scene seemingly untouched by the relentless march of time.

Once a bustling thoroughfare, the central path was now dedicated to pedestrians while vendors hawked their wares from their brightly lit alcoves. Narrow alleyways snaked off like inquisitive serpents, promising hidden treasures and clandestine deals for those who dared to venture into their depths.

Rye was assaulted by a hit of vivid memories.

"This is exactly as I was," he murmured to Isis, a tremor of wonder lacing his voice.

The chaos of the marketplace assailed his senses. Fabrics of every imaginable hue and texture adorned the stalls – simple, utilitarian garments intermingled with luxurious silks and intricately embroidered gowns, each a testament to the artistry on display. Cell phones, with their aggressively bright displays and garish plastic shells, seemed like jarring intruders in this timeless setting.

With his heightened awareness, Rye found them almost distasteful – cheap baubles compared to the craftsmanship and timeless elegance he remembered.

Still, he approached a seller.

"Hello, how are you?" he asked.

"Greetings, doing very fine here. What can I help you with?" the seller responded.

"I am looking for a timepiece. A digital one," Rye replied.

Acknowledging Rye's attitude with a brisk nod, the vendor boomed, "Ah, a timepiece you seek! Look no further, my friend. Here's how to find what you desire. Head past my humble stall and down the path until you reach the third turn on your right. Take that turn and proceed straight ahead. Then, take the second left, and you'll find yourself amidst a bounty of watch merchants and their pre-packaged wares."

"Thank you kindly," Rye replied, a genuine appreciation warming his voice.

As they started their journey deeper into the market, Rye turned to Isis, his mind buzzing with newfound insights.

"This is truly remarkable," he confessed. "The more I see, the more I'm inclined to believe history is a circle, and our lives are reflections of that cycle. We may not be the same people reborn, but perhaps the essence remains – the same outlook, the same drive, maybe even the spark of the same soul."

Isis, with her eyes gleaming with an otherworldly intelligence, responded telepathically.

"Losing one's soul... it's not an experience I've had, but I understand it's a possibility. Perhaps life and karma are closer to a Mobius Strip, an endless loop with no true beginning or end. In this view, Earth becomes a harsh learning ground, dense and slow-moving compared to other planes. Here, thoughts manifest with a kind of friction. Victories and losses feel more tangible. It's a crucible, a place to experiment with spirituality or to choose a path free from such constraints."

Rye followed the directions the seller gave to him, gently weaving through the throngs of people and past stalls overflowing with vibrant wares. Finally, they reached a turn marked by a discreet sign that read "Watches" in faded Arabic script. Relief washed over him – here, nestled beneath a hand-built shingled overhang, was a haven of timepieces.

"This should be it," Rye said to Isis, drawing her attention to the place.

The stall was adorned with strings of LED lights that cast a festive glow on the diverse array of watches displayed. Circular and partially circular designs dominated, each vying for Rye's attention. A man with a weathered face and eyes that sparkled with the cunning of a seasoned merchant approached them with a warm smile.

"Welcome! Can I be of assistance in finding the perfect timepiece?"

"Indeed, I hope so," Rye replied, his gaze sweeping across the collection. "I'm on the lookout for a digital watch, one with a satellite connection and solar charging capabilities."

The merchant's smile widened.

"Excellent choice, sir! You're in luck. I have three different models that fit your requirements."

He glanced at Isis, a flicker of amusement dancing in his eyes, then back to Rye with a knowing wink.

"Serendipity, perhaps?"

Rye couldn't help but return the gesture. Three options, just as he'd intuitively felt.

There was a bright yellow model, but using his ESP, Rye bypassed it in favor of the one nestled beside it. This one, crafted from sleek steel and boasting a cool grey finish, seemed to resonate with him. A closer inspection confirmed his instincts – it displayed time and date and had a satellite connection. It housed a stopwatch function, could track his location, and even contained downloadable maps!

Not only was it waterproof, but it also boasted an impressive feature – the ability to detect approaching storms. And, crucially, it drew power from the very sun that beat down on the bustling marketplace.

"That's it," Rye murmured to Isis, a hint of satisfaction tinging his voice. Turning back to the vendor, he confirmed his choice.

"Yes, sir, I'll take this one," he declared, holding up the grey watch.

"Excellent selection, sir!" the owner boomed, his voice thick with genuine enthusiasm. "A sturdy watch indeed, known to last a lifetime, or close to it."

"Perfect," Rye replied with a grin.

Durability was exactly what he craved.

The owner deftly placed the watch in a small bag, and the transaction was complete.

"That'll be £10,000," he announced.

Rye counted out the exact amount in bills, his movements practiced.

"Here you go," he said, handing over the money.

"Thank you kindly, sir," the owner responded, his smile widening. "May it serve you well. Take care now."

Rye returned the sentiment, a sense of satisfaction warming him. This watch was more than just a timepiece – it was a marvel of technology, a fusion of function and practicality. As he slipped it onto his left wrist, he marveled at its additional features – heart rate monitor and blood pressure readings! It was like having a miniaturized medical tricorder strapped to his arm.

"This is fantastic," he murmured to Isis, a hint of awe in his voice. "It even does vitals! Exactly what I was hoping for."

Taking a few steps away from the stall, Rye inspected the watch with renewed interest, his ESP granting him an extra layer of insight. He read the time displayed.

"It's 11:24."

A soft chuckle escaped Isis' lips.

"Alright, Captain Caveman," she teased telepathically. "Ready to explore some more? Or are you content, marveling at your new gadget?"

Rye's brow furrowed in mock offense.

"Captain Caveman?" he repeated with a playful glint in his eyes. "Who exactly is the caveman here? The one who can barely navigate time or the one who can read minds?"

Their quiet browsing was shattered by a sudden commotion emanating from beyond the watch booth. A harsh cry of "Yusaeid!" – a plea for help – pierced the air, drawing Rye and Isis's attention like a magnet.

Hurriedly, they navigated the collection of people, their eyes scanning for the source of the distress. They arrived at a scene that sent anger through Rye. A large, sweaty man towered over another figure crumpled on the dusty ground. With a sickening thud, the larger man delivered a final kick to the fallen man's stomach, his voice laced with venom.

"Get out of my space! Go!" he roared.

The man on the ground, his clothes barely clinging to his emaciated frame, whimpered in pain. This wasn't a fight; it was a brutal display of dominance.

"Breaking his finger was being 'nice.' I told him I'd do it if he came back," the large man sneered, his words dripping with malice.

Rye's jaw clenched. He locked eyes with Isis, a silent communication passing between them.

"We'll get him a taxi," Rye declared, his voice firm yet calm. He addressed the hulking figure, his gaze unwavering. "Be at peace."

The large man scoffed.

"Peace? I can't have him loitering around here. Bad for business!" he gestured dismissively toward the injured man.

Disgusted, Rye turned away from the bully and knelt beside the injured man. Isis was already there; her touch was calm as she assessed the damage.

Isis sent a telepathic message to Rye.

"He has a badly broken and crushed leg. He says he just wants to work but can't afford surgery."

Without hesitation, Isis placed her hands on the man's injured leg, her eyes glowing with a faint inner light. Understanding her unspoken request, Rye followed suit, placing his hands on the man's temples. A surge of energy crackled between them, a silent plea for healing coursing through their veins. Their actions were shrouded in a mystical veil thanks to Isis' magic.

The transformation was swift and awe-inspiring. The man's broken leg was mended, the telltale signs of malnutrition vanished, and his tattered clothes were replaced with clean, functional garments.

Isis lifted her hands, a satisfied smile gracing her lips.

"It is complete. Fully restored."

The man, bewildered by the miraculous turn of events, stammered, "I, I don't know what to say... You are very special. I will never forget what you've done for me. Thank you a thousand times!"

"What's your name?" Rye asked gently.

"Nasir," he replied, his voice filled with newfound hope.

"I'm Rye," Rye said, extending his hand to help him. "And before you go, I want you to have this."

He reached into his pocket and pressed a gold coin into Nasir's palm.

"A little something to get you started on a new job," Rye added, his gaze locking with Nasir's. "Not here."

Nasir gaped at the gold coin, its weight a stark contrast to the emptiness of his pockets.

"Sir, I couldn't possibly take this," he stammered, his voice thick with emotion. "This is… massive."

Rye pressed the coin firmly into Nasir's hand, his gaze unwavering.

"Use it wisely," he said. "A little at a time, but I want you to have it."

Nasir's eyes welled up with tears.

"How could I ever repay you?" he sobbed.

"By making a dream come true," Rye replied, a gentle smile on his lips. "You mentioned a bakery... something you yearn for. This can be your seed money. Your chance to create your own space, to rise above your circumstances."

Nasir's face lit up, a spark of hope igniting in his eyes.

"My own bakery? You believe in me?"

"Absolutely," Rye affirmed with conviction. "Now, let's get you out of here."

All three walked past the large, sweaty man, who remained blissfully unaware of their presence thanks to Isis's magic. They ascended a small step, seemingly teleporting a short distance down the walkway. In that imperceptible blink, they shifted back into the physical plane, leaving Nasir slightly bewildered but none the worse for wear.

"My heartfelt thanks to both of you," Nasir said, his voice thick with gratitude. "That was... special. Unexplainable! And you've given me more than I could ever ask for. May peace and harmony forever bless your paths."

As Nasir hailed a taxi, they all exchanged a wave – a silent farewell before Isis and Rye slipped into the inviting darkness of an alleyway.

"Whew, that was incredible," Rye breathed, his voice tinged with awe. "You were brilliant, Isis. A true healer."

Isis responded telepathically, a warmth radiating from her presence.

"Indeed, each encounter holds its significance. And to you, very nice work. You provided the spark of hope, the encouragement he needed to believe in himself."

Rye chuckled, a playful glint in his eyes.

"So, Captain Caveman isn't so bad after all, eh?"

Isis' smile widened as she burst into laughter.

"Captain Caveman," she echoed, shaking her head. "It seems I have much to learn about you, my friend. A journey that promises to be long and filled with laughter."

Rye joined in her laughter, a sense of camaraderie blossoming between them. This was just the beginning, he knew. Their adventure in Khan el-Khalili had only begun, and the mysteries that awaited them were as vast and vibrant as the marketplace itself.

Chapter 7

"That healing definitely drained me," Rye admitted to Isis, his voice slightly strained.

Isis, ever perceptive, nodded in understanding.

"Using your energy to mend another can be quite taxing, especially in the beginning."

She gestured toward the bustling marketplace around them.

"How about we find a place to rest and recharge? Perhaps a cup of coffee?"

"Perfect," Rye agreed, a grateful smile flickering across his lips.

They continued their exploration, drawn by the enticing aromas wafted from various stalls. Deeper within the heart of the marketplace, they stumbled upon a cluster of inviting cafes, their warm lighting beckoning weary travelers. Settling at a small table for two, they awaited their server's arrival.

"Isis," Rye began, his gaze sweeping over the scene. "What is the history behind this coffee they serve here?"

"Kahwa," Isis replied, a hint of amusement in her voice. "It's a traditional beverage, steeped in history."

A young waiter approached their table, his smile as warm as the surrounding ambiance. Isis placed her order first.

"Kahwa, please," she requested.

Rye followed suit.

"Two kahwas, thank you," he confirmed.

"Certainly," the waiter replied, his voice polite and efficient, before disappearing back into the bustling cafe.

"Coffee has always held a special significance for different cultures," Rye mused, continuing his earlier train of thought. "Even in my time, each region had its own unique brewing rituals and traditions. It seems that hasn't changed a bit."

A soft chuckle escaped Rye's lips.

"There's something undeniably humorous about it, wouldn't you agree?" he said, referring to the relentless pursuit of the perfect cup of coffee across cultures. "The lengths we go to, the rituals we create..."

He knew Isis possessed the answer to any question he might pose, but that wasn't the point. Their connection transcended mere information retrieval. Here, on Earth, they cherished the experience, the shared journey of discovery. Questions could wait; reveling in the present was what truly mattered.

The waiter returned, balancing a tray laden with two steaming cups of coffee.

"Many thanks," Rye acknowledged with a nod.

"So," he began, laying out a plan for the remainder of their day. "Perhaps we spend the rest of today navigating and locating some maps. Then, tomorrow, I'd love to visit Mal and Ena, my light vampires. I've been yearning to see them since awakening."

He turned to Isis, his gaze filled with warmth.

"Would you care to join me?"

Isis' telepathic response resonated with a profound sense of joy.

"Absolutely," she echoed. "Wherever your path leads, that's where I want to be."

A thoughtful pause followed.

"If you'd like," she continued. "I can inform the other deities of my whereabouts. They can take a temporary leave of absence but remain on standby, ready to intervene if needed."

"Excellent suggestion," Rye replied, his voice laced with approval. "Yes, I like that very much. Knowing the others are aware and available for a moment's notice provides a sense of comfort."

A sly grin tugged at the corner of his lips.

"Besides, I can only imagine their intrigue regarding tomorrow night's encounter with Ammit."

The mere mention of the devourer of souls sent a flicker of anticipation through him.

Isis' telepathic message resonated with a note of concern.

"Never far apart, yes?" she probed, sensing the shift in Rye's demeanor.

Rye shook his head slightly, dispelling any misconception.

"Not in the romantic sense, Isis," he clarified. "This is a battle we face, a shift in the very fabric of reality. Tonight, I must connect with the Star Beings and our allies, the Zetas. We need a unified front."

His voice took on a grave tone.

"There's only one Ammit and only one Set, but the chaos they can unleash is immeasurable. The question remains: how do we neutralize Set? He'll stop at nothing to claim the Ka sword."

Isis listened intently, her brow furrowing in concentration.

"He's impervious to mortal weapons," she confirmed, her voice laced with concern. "But there's a chance divine armaments can inflict harm."

Chapter 8

Rye drained the last of his coffee, the bitter dregs mirroring the seriousness of their situation.

"What if," he began, his voice low and rumbling. "We had five light vampires, each wielding a spear?"

Isis leaned forward, her eyes gleaming, echoing his growing urgency.

"An interesting proposition. Spears, imbued with what?"

"The violet flame," Rye replied, his gaze hardening with resolve. "Channeled through each spear with all the collective power we can muster. All aimed at a single, precise target – Set's midsection."

"Set's god-like nature renders him impervious to mortal weapons. However, a divine weapon infused with the violet flame..." her voice trailed off, the possibilities swirling in her mind like smoke rising from a sacrificial fire.

"Could be the key to disrupting his form, weakening him enough to separate him from the Ka sword," Rye finished her thought.

As audacious as it was, the plan wasn't without its complexities. Five light vampires, chosen for their unwavering loyalty and unwavering strength, would be the instruments of this attack. Each spear, crafted from a celestial metal known only to a select few, must be meticulously prepared to channel the violet flame's potent energy.

A heavy silence descended upon them as the weight of their task settled in. This wasn't just about strategy; it was about sacrifice. The violet flame, a potent weapon against the forces of darkness, could also exact a toll on its wielders. Despite their enhanced nature, the light vampires wouldn't be immune to its draining effects.

"We can't risk their well-being without proper preparation," Rye declared, his voice firm and with unwavering resolve. "They'll need to do some rigorous training – mental and physical – to handle the power that they're channeling."

Isis, her brow furrowed in concentration, closed her eyes and reached out with her telepathic senses.

"Agreed. I can initiate contact with Star Beings. Perhaps they have insights on how to fortify the light vampires and enhance the spears' potency."

The Star Beings, ancient celestial entities with a wellspring of knowledge, might be the missing piece in their plan. Their guidance and Isis' formidable powers could make the difference between success and failure.

Then, a ghost of a smile played on Rye's lips.

"Perhaps we've gotten a little too serious," he chuckled, the tension momentarily broken. "We still have time before the inevitable confrontation. Time to strategize, to gather our allies, and maybe even... relax a little."

Isis, mirroring his smile, couldn't help but agree. They needed this stolen moment of normalcy amidst the looming chaos.

"To relaxation, then," she said, raising an empty cup in a mock toast. "And to trusting the flow of events, as serious as they may be."

Isis' telepathic reply resonated within Rye's mind.

"I agree. Everything is in its right place. A calmness before the storm, perhaps?"

Rye chuckled, a low rumble in his chest.

"Perhaps," he conceded, finishing the last of his coffee. He signaled for the waiter, laying down a generous payment on the table.

"All finished?" he inquired, the question directed both at Isis and the approaching server.

A reassuring warmth filled him as Isis responded, "Yes, and feeling fine. Ready to delve into the maps."

"Excellent," Rye replied with a genuine smile. "Then let's see what the marketplace holds for us."

Public displays of affection were a tightrope walk in this part of the world, a consequence of the prevailing Muslim beliefs. Understanding this unspoken rule, Rye and Isis refrained from any physical contact as they rose from their table. Instead, they turned back toward the bustling heart of the marketplace. Their movements were a silent conversation in itself.

The air was filled with the intoxicating aroma of spices as they navigated through narrow tunnels. Lanterns, their warm glow casting dancing shadows on the stone walls, illuminated their path. Colorful displays lined the walkways –overflowing fruit baskets, worn leather backpacks, weathered journals, and stalls brimming with steaming coffee pots.

Their steps slowed as they passed a particularly captivating display of intricately crafted lanterns. Unable to resist his curiosity, Rye approached the young man tending the stall.

"Excuse me," he began politely. "Could you point us toward some maps?"

The young man, his smile as bright as the lanterns themselves, gestured toward the throng of people ahead.

"Up closer to the front, sir! You can't miss them."

"Much appreciated," Rye replied, a courteous nod accompanying his words.

He turned back to Isis, a familiar wave of awe washing over him as he met her gaze.

'How,' he thought not for the first time. *'Had fate brought him back to her side?'*

Their connection transcended mere chance; it felt preordained, like a cosmic thread weaving them together.

The marketplace had swelled considerably, a reflection of the Thursday afternoon tradition. Many locals enjoyed a half-day work schedule, savoring a taste of freedom before the weekend truly began. The crowd pulsed with energy. There was a symphony of haggling voices and the rhythmic thump of music drifting from a nearby stall.

Rye and Isis navigated the throng, their movements a well-rehearsed dance. Squeezing past a vendor hawking carpets, they finally emerged in a more open area. A booth overflowing with maps and guidebooks caught Rye's eye.

He approached with a quickened pace, his enhanced senses activating. A pulse of electricity ran through him as he scanned the map displayed prominently at the front – a world map. Egypt, Africa, Antarctica – the names of continents laid before his inner vision. Beyond that, a glimpse of familiar lands – the United Kingdom, Denmark, Sweden, Italy, Greece.

So many places, so many people. The world, vast and teeming with life, stretched out before him on that single sheet of paper. A pang of longing, a whisper of adventures past, flickered in his chest.

But for now, the present demanded his focus. He reached out, selecting the world map and a hefty guidebook dedicated to Alexandria. The shopkeeper, a wizened man with eyes as crinkled as the papyrus scrolls stacked behind him, beamed.

The transaction was swift, a cordial exchange of words and coins. As Rye and Isis stepped back into the bright Egyptian sunlight, a sigh of contentment escaped his lips. Few things, he realized, held the same power as the warmth of the Egyptian sun on his skin. It was a familiar embrace, a connection that resonated deep within his being.

A slow smile spread across Rye's face as he turned to Isis. Her form seemed to shimmer with an ethereal light, a reflection of his contentment.

"I think we made it, sir," her telepathic message resonated within him, laced with amusement.

Rye chuckled, the sound low and warm.

"I do believe you're right, little miss," he replied, using a term Thoth's hoop had brought back to him – a term that felt faintly antiquated yet strangely fitting in the present moment. "The sunlight does feel good, doesn't it?"

He reached out, hailing a taxi with a practiced gesture honed from centuries of traversing the globe. The vehicle, a dented but reliable-looking yellow cab, screeched to a stop before them. With a flourish, Rye opened the passenger door, gesturing for Isis to enter.

As she settled gracefully into the worn leather seat, Rye slid beside her and shut the door.

"To the Steigenberger Hotel, please," he instructed the driver, his voice firm yet polite.

"Righty-o," the driver replied with a thick Egyptian accent. "That'll be 40 pounds."

Rye, his mind still adjusting to the local currency thanks to Thoth's influence, fumbled slightly for the correct amount. He finally retrieved a £40 note and, on a whim, added an extra £20.

The car lurched forward, joining the throng of vehicles navigating the bustling streets. As the city blurred past the window, Rye reached out telepathically to Isis.

"I don't know that we'll always be confined to Alexandria," he admitted. "I never intended for us to stay put. Back in the day, Mal and Ena weren't exactly homebodies either. The world has a lot to offer, and now..."

He trailed off, his gaze flickering with a hint of mischief.

"I would love to travel with you, anywhere, anywhere at all," her reply echoed in his mind, filled with a feeling that mirrored his own burgeoning sense of adventure.

Rye couldn't help but smile. With its unexpected twists and turns, this journey was proving to be far more exhilarating than he'd ever anticipated. And with Isis by his side, he knew they could face whatever challenges awaited them anywhere in this vast and wondrous world.

Chapter 9

The taxi screeched to a halt with a final cough of its engine, pulling up right in front of the Steigenberger Hotel's imposing entrance. Rye turned to the driver, a smile playing on his lips.

"Thank you, sir," he said, his voice laced with appreciation. "Much obliged."

The driver, a weathered man with a sun-baked face, returned the smile with a nod.

"Any time, friend," he replied, his thick accent adding a touch of warmth to his words. "Call on me whenever you need a ride around the city."

With a wave and a final shift of gears, the taxi dissolved into a throng of vehicles, leaving Rye and Isis on the bustling sidewalk.

Isis tilted her head, her brow furrowing slightly.

"What time is it?" she inquired, a hint of playfulness peeking through her telepathic message.

Rye chuckled, his enhanced senses picking up the subtle shift in her mood.

"Almost four o'clock," he replied, consulting the elegant timepiece Thoth's hoop had subtly replaced on his wrist.

A mischievous glint sparked in his eyes.

"We could spend some time enjoying the view from the rooftop," he suggested.

Isis' telepathic response resonated with delight.

"That would be splendid. A chance to gather our thoughts and soak in the city's vibrant energy."

"Agreed," Rye confirmed. He gestured toward a discreet side entrance tucked away from the main flow of foot traffic. "The rooftop terrace overlooks the city, but it's a fair climb. Probably best for us to remain invisible, considering the daylight and all those windows."

With a knowing nod, Isis brushed her fingers against his arm. A faint tingling sensation washed over Rye, followed by the exhilarating feeling of his physical form dissolving into a state of invisibility.

A silent smile played on his lips as he led the way, his senses heightened by his enhanced abilities. Together, they slipped past the unsuspecting hotel staff and ascended the winding staircase, their destination: a hidden oasis above the bustling city, a place to strategize, reconnect, and face the coming challenges with a united front.

As they reached the secluded side entrance, a mischievous twinkle danced in Isis' eyes.

"Come on over here," she murmured telepathically, a playful smile gracing her lips.

Rye's heart skipped a beat. He couldn't resist the invitation in her eyes. With a knowing smirk, he closed the distance between them, his hands finding their place on her back. The world around them seemed to shimmer, then dissolve entirely as they embraced the invisibility granted by Thoth's gift.

The sudden weightlessness that followed made Rye grin. Invisibility was one thing, but the ability to phase through solid objects –was a different kind of thrill entirely.

Isis' voice, light and teasing, echoed in his mind.

"Now this is interesting… We don't have to go to the hotel roof, do we? Want to fly some?"

The notion sent a jolt of excitement through him.

"Let's go for it!" he replied, his voice filled with an eager anticipation.

He felt her body tense slightly as she prepared for liftoff. Instinctively, he tightened his grip around her, the familiar warmth of her form a reassuring presence. Then, with a gentle whoosh of displaced air, they were airborne.

The cityscape unfolded beneath them, a breathtaking tapestry of bustling streets, towering buildings, and the shimmering Nile River snaking through the heart of Alexandria. The wind whipped through Rye's hair, carrying the sounds of the city – a symphony of honking horns, laughter, and distant music.

They soared effortlessly, hugging the vertical surface of the Steigenberger Hotel. Isis' movements were graceful, her body gliding through the air like a bird returning home. Each brush of her wings sent a thrill through Rye, a mix of exhilaration and awe at the goddess by his side.

Finally, they reached the rooftop, hovering several feet above its surface. The city lights, twinkling on in the approaching dusk, painted the scene with a magical glow. The cool evening air caressed their faces, carrying the scent of spices and jasmine.

Rye loosened his grip slightly, gazing out at the sprawling panorama.

"This view," he breathed, his voice tinged with wonder. "It is even more spectacular from up here."

A wave of delight washed over Rye at hearing Isis' words.

"I remember! I remember!" he exclaimed, a surge of nostalgia coursing through him. "Flying together – what a joy and a thrill. Yes, let's!"

Their connection deepened as they clasped onto each other, a silent understanding passing between them. Isis sent a questioning message.

"Which way?"

His gaze drawn magnetically toward the west, Rye pointed toward the horizon.

"The Mediterranean," he declared, his voice laced with excitement. "Let's fly toward the vastness of the sea."

They launched forward with a burst of shared energy fueled by exuberance and the thrill of flight. Gone was the tentative hovering; their movements were now a coordinated dance, their combined power propelling them with exhilarating speed. The cityscape receded behind them, replaced by the endless expanse of the Mediterranean Sea.

The turquoise water stretched out before them like a giant, glittering jewel, the setting sun casting a golden glow upon its surface. White-capped waves danced and frolicked, their rhythmic crashes a soothing counterpoint to the rush of wind against their invisible forms.

A cry of pure joy escaped Rye's lips as he soared, his arms outstretched, drinking in the breathtaking vista. Isis, mirroring his exhilaration, let out a peal of celestial laughter that echoed across the ocean's vastness.

As they reached the curved edge of the coastline, the city lights twinkled like fallen stars on the horizon.

"Let's fly out over the water," Rye suggested, his voice filled with an adventurous spirit.

Isis' telepathic response echoed with a playful lilt.

"Alright," she agreed, and with a coordinated dip and turn, they banked sharply, carving a wide arc out over the vast expanse of the Mediterranean.

The wind whipped through their invisible forms, carrying the ocean's salty spray. Below them, the waves rolled and churned, dwarfed by the sheer immensity of the sea.

A surge of adventurous spirit coursed through Rye. He leaned into the wind, his voice tinged with excitement.

"We could even fly all the way across to Italy!" he exclaimed, the world suddenly feeling impossibly small beneath their soaring forms.

Isis dipped her head, her laughter echoing in his mind. "Rye, there is no limit, no parameters other than if you get tired. And there is this," she added, hovering mid-air.

Before he could react, she leaned in, her lips brushing his neck in intimate and playful gestures. The touch sent a jolt of electricity through him, a reminder of their powerful connection.

"And the secret is, it is boundless," she concluded, her voice laced with a hint of amusement.

Rye felt a wave of warmth wash over him.

"How I'd forgotten," he murmured, his voice thick with emotion. "Forgotten the exhilaration of flight, the freedom of the open sky. And here you are, reminding me."

A look of determination hardened his features.

"We have a purpose, Isis, a battle to face. But before we confront Ammit," he continued, his gaze fixed on the horizon. "We could head south and see where I'm destined to meet her."

Isis tilted her head, her eyes gleaming with a shared resolve.

"Okay, I'm up for it. Let's see where destiny leads us. Together."

With a renewed sense of purpose and a shared love for adventure, they dove back toward the Egyptian coastline, the vastness of the Mediterranean Sea their playground, and the confrontation with Ammit, a looming shadow on the horizon.

A silent understanding passed between them in response to Isis' whisper.

"Let's get going…"

Rye tightened his grip around her as they embraced, their invisible forms rising higher into the twilight sky. Wrapped together in a cocoon of shared energy, they accelerated, the wind a symphony in his ears. This was pure, unadulterated freedom, a release from the weight of the world and the burdens they carried.

He held her close, her back pressed against his chest, as they soared toward the waterfront. Then, with a graceful dip and turn, they curved right, following the glittering ribbon of the Mediterranean south.

"If we follow Highway 40, it will take us to our destination," Isis' voice resonated in his mind, laced with amusement. "And you'll get to see a lot of cars."

Rye glanced at the clock hovering on his wrist, courtesy of Thoth's ever-evolving influence. It was just approaching 5:45 pm.

"Sounds like a plan," he replied telepathically. "Let's see what kind of traffic Egypt offers."

With a subtle shift, they veered slightly left. Below them, the asphalt ribbon of Highway 40 stretched out like a shimmering scar across the landscape. Vehicles of all shapes and sizes zipped along it – sleek sedans, sturdy trucks, rumbling motorcycles, and lumbering semi-trucks. Yet, they flew effortlessly past them all, their speed starkly contrasting the mundane reality unfolding beneath them.

An unexpected sensation washed over Rye – his eyes, unaccustomed to the wind at such velocity, began to water. He blinked, realizing with amusement that perhaps he needed to acquire more practical eyewear. After millennia, certain human limitations still held a touch of novelty.

"Think Thoth's hoop could manage some… flying goggles?" he murmured telepathically to Isis, a hint of amusement in his voice.

Navigating the skies with less watery eyes held a certain appeal.

They skimmed the highway, the roar of the engines and the acrid bite of exhaust fumes starkly contrasting with the serenity of their flight. Bound together, they resembled a single, ethereal entity gliding effortlessly above the throng of vehicles. Below them, the modern-day "camels," as Rye mused, weaved a ceaseless dance of commerce, transporting their loads across the vast expanse of the desert.

A nudge from Isis drew his attention to the left. There, bathed in the soft glow of the approaching twilight, lay the unmistakable ruins of Taposiris Magna. Isis, her voice filled with awe, echoed his thoughts.

"These are indeed the ruins from the Ptolemaic dynasty. Some say Cleopatra herself is buried deep down here, and some are still searching for her secrets."

With a silent agreement, they unwound from their embrace, their invisible forms hovering silently above the ancient city. The wind whispered through the weathered stones, carrying the weight of history. These were the remnants of a glorious civilization, a testament to the power and ingenuity of a bygone era.

The ruins, bathed in the ethereal glow of twilight, presented a captivating sight. Large, toppled columns dominated the landscape, their fallen forms a poignant reminder of the passage of time. Broken blocks of stone, jagged remnants of walls long since crumbled, lay scattered like discarded toys. Whipped by the ceaseless desert wind, sand painted the ruins with a timeless patina.

Rye and Isis descended, settling gracefully onto the sandy ground at the heart of the ruins. The silence here was profound, broken only by the sighing of the wind and the occasional rustle of displaced sand. A sense of anticipation settled over them – this was the place, the stage upon which the world's fate might very well be decided.

"Okay," Rye murmured, his voice tinged with a quiet resolve. "Tomorrow at midnight. Here."

He cast a glance around the sprawling ruins, the weight of the coming confrontation settling on him.

"Will you be here, too?" he asked, a note of concern creeping into his voice.

Isis' telepathic response was a gentle brush against his mind.

"No, the Enneads asked me to meet you afterward. It is mostly the pitched battle you will set up. They will provide reinforcements when the time comes."

Rye nodded, a flicker of understanding passing through him.

"Understood," he replied.

He bent down, picking up a medium-sized piece of sandstone, its surface smooth and worn by time.

"Ah, a rock hound, too?" Isis teased, her voice laced with amusement.

A wry smile touched Rye's lips.

"I remember that as well," he admitted. "I had quite a collection back in the day. This was before…"

His voice trailed off, a hint of nostalgia tingeing his tone.

"Before I met you, as you are now. I even had a shrine set up for the Egyptian gods and goddesses. One for you, of course. Little did I know I'd be flying around with you like this."

A thoughtful expression crossed his face.

"Do the others, the Enneads, know about us?" he inquired, curiosity getting the better of him.

"They do in their own way," Isis replied sagely. "They approve, but we are granted our privacy. It's a delicate balance."

"Well, that's certainly kind of them," Rye chuckled, a sense of relief washing over him. "Want to head back to the hotel? Considering the day we've had, I think a decent night's sleep might be in order."

Isis' amusement was palpable.

"I do. We can go invisible over 40, above, and head-on. A quick and easy flight."

"Sounds like a plan," Rye agreed.

He reached out, taking her hand in his. Together, they rose slowly from the ancient ruins, their forms shimmering as they cloaked themselves in invisibility.

With a silent understanding, they flew north, the vast expanse of the silent Mediterranean Sea now a dark presence on their left. The desert wind whipped past them, carrying the whispers of the past.

"How fast can we go?" Rye asked, a hint of a challenge in his voice. The prospect of a high-speed flight back to the hotel held a certain appeal.

A knowing smile played on Isis' lips as she sent her response.

"If we were higher, we could break the sound barrier. But you're right, that would be a tad dramatic for our current audience down there."

They skimmed the vehicles' rooftops on Highway 40, their invisible forms a blur against the twilight sky. The rhythmic hum of traffic and the distant glow of the city lights painted a surreal scene below them.

"Here comes the hotel," Rye announced, pointing toward the Steigenberger's imposing silhouette rising from the cityscape.

A mischievous glint sparked in his eyes.

"Let's do a loop for old time's sake," he suggested, a playful edge creeping into his voice.

Isis' telepathic response was a delighted, "Okay, sure!"

They soared in a wide arc, a silent ballet against the backdrop of the Egyptian night sky. Pulling a tight loop, they skimmed the side of the hotel wall before gracefully landing on the flat rooftop.

A surge of energy crackled between them as their invisible forms brushed against each other. They stood for a moment, their embrace a silent language that spoke volumes. Then, with a gentle murmur, they pulled apart.

A soft smile touched Rye's lips as he brushed a cheek against hers, their connection unspoken yet profound.

"Now," he murmured. "If memory serves, this would be a good time to connect with our allies."

Isis nodded, her eyes gleaming with understanding.

Taking a deep breath, Rye focused his mental energies. He projected a potent thought construct, a tightly woven bubble of information encompassing everything he knew about Ammit, Set, and the brewing conflict. The construct contained details of their motivations, strengths, and weaknesses – a complete picture of the threat they faced.

The understanding was instantaneous. Thought constructs, complex packets of information, transcended the need for spoken language. The message shot out, reaching the Pleiadians, Arcturians, and Sirians with pinpoint accuracy.

At that moment, Rye knew they were received. He closed the construct with a mental coda – a promise to update them after he meets with Ammit to share the details of the confrontation and the enemy's state.

A sense of quiet satisfaction settled over him. They weren't alone in this fight. The Star Beings, bound by their shared interest in protecting the universe's balance, would be watching, waiting to offer their support when the time came.

"That should do the trick," Rye affirmed, a flicker of relief crossing his features.

Telepathy, the language of the cosmos, offered a level of efficiency unmatched by any human communication method. He turned to Isis, a confident glint in his eye.

Isis tilted her head, her brow arched in a question. Her telepathic inquiry resonated within him.

"Did they receive it?"

A satisfied smile spread across Rye's face.

"Rye, I just got a response," he projected telepathically. "All three groups will be in their orbs. That's very beneficial. They're already preparing."

A low hum of approval emanated from Isis. The Star Beings' swift response boded well for the coming battle.

Rye took a moment to explain the nature of the orbs for Isis' benefit.

"Orbs," he explained telepathically. "These come in various sizes, ranging from an ant's brain to a large tractor-trailer. They usually appear about the size of a soccer ball, as they find it less intrusive or shocking to humans. They can fire powerful energy beams – violet flames roughly the size and shape of a large drinking glass – in rapid succession. These orbs are usually glowing and float around but can also reach high planes of existence."

With a glance at his wrist, courtesy of Thoth's ever-evolving influence, Rye noted the approaching hour.

"It's nearly seven o'clock," he murmured. "I need to contact the Zetas next because they operate a little differently."

He straightened his stance, a determined expression settling on his face. Closing his eyes, he mimicked the process used for the previous thought constructs, channeling his message with laser-like focus. This time, however, the message was specifically addressed to his friend Hal.

"Hal," Rye projected mentally, his voice filled with quiet urgency. "We need your help. Ammit has returned, and we're facing a showdown at the ruins of Taposiris Magna tomorrow night. Meet us there – in spirit if not in body. We could use your expertise."

He paused, allowing the message to hang in the air momentarily.

"And Hal," he added, a warmth creeping into his voice. "Good to be back in touch, old friend."

With that, he opened his eyes, a flicker of anticipation mingling with the ever-present weight of responsibility on his features. He turned to Isis, his gaze seeking hers.

"The Zetas operate differently," he explained. "They don't use orbs but can project themselves across vast distances in spirit form. Hopefully, Hal will receive the message."

A wave of relief washed over Rye as Hal's telepathic response flooded his mind. The Zetas, his bionic grey friends, were on their way.

"Zeta Reticuli, indeed," Rye murmured, a hint of a smile on his lips. "The Greys. Good to know it's the real deal and not those darn robotic imposters they keep getting mixed up with."

Hal's message painted a vivid picture – a ship being readied, a force assembled. The sheer efficiency of the Zetas was both reassuring and slightly intimidating.

"That's fine, just fine," Rye projected back telepathically.

"And yes, Hal," he added with a chuckle. "I'm still getting used to the new world myself. Everything is so much more advanced than I remember!"

Hal's amusement was palpable.

"Yessir, it's great to know you've been found and uncovered," he responded. "All of your Zeta friends are glad to hear this news. Keep recharging, and I'm sure you'll find other abilities. There's a lot to see in Alexandria, and even more across Egypt, even though things have changed a bit."

Rye grimaced slightly.

"Yes," he admitted, a touch of sadness tinging his voice. "Much was broken down in the 1400s when I was last here. I can only faintly remember anything before then."

"Maybe visiting these places can help jog your memory," Hal suggested helpfully. "Yessir, indeed. I would recommend revisiting your old stomping grounds. They're still unearthing artifacts and forgotten dynastic pieces even now."

A spark of interest ignited in Rye's eyes.

"Even though my last home was in Alexandria," he replied. "I lived in Memphis, Thebes, and Luxor before."

"Yessir," Hal confirmed. "I'd suggest you visit your old haunts. They continue to dig up artifacts and long-hidden dynastic pieces even these days. It won't take long for me to gather this Zeta force, and then we'll rendezvous with you – out in orbit."

Rye nodded, a sense of purpose solidifying within him.

"Okay, my friend. One more day to go, then the midnight meeting with Ammit."

He glanced at Isis, who was gazing out at the cityscape with a thoughtful expression.

"Tomorrow, I plan to visit Mal and Ena," he continued, his voice laced with a hint of apprehension. "I haven't contacted them yet. Then, after I address this Ammit situation, I can explore Memphis and the others. Perhaps revisiting those places will indeed jog some memories."

"Yessir," Hal concluded, his tone filled with encouragement. "I think you'll be pleasantly surprised."

As the telepathic connection faded, a wave of determination settled over Rye. He had allies, both old and new, standing beside him. With their combined strength, he was ready to face whatever Ammit and Set threw his way.

A smile touched Rye's lips as he projected his response to Hal.

"That would be great, Hal. I'm truly glad to reconnect with you after all this time and all that's happened. You always have a way of helping me see the bigger picture."

Hal's reply resonated with a hint of pride.

"Yessir, we've undergone several changes and upgrades since your time in the 1400s. Our numbers have grown significantly, along with our larger ships and the frequency of our visits to Earth. We remain steadfast in our mission as peacekeepers, and we've gained many allies in the process."

Rye chuckled inwardly. He'd tried to dissuade Hal from using the honorific "sir," but the designation seemed ingrained in the Zeta's programming. It held a certain charm, a reminder of their long friendship.

"I'm honored to be working with you again, Hal," Rye projected telepathically. "And speaking of working together, I have a question for you."

He cast a glance around the rooftop, his senses sweeping outwards. No malevolent entities were present – the rooftop remained a haven for their conversation.

Sensing his inquiry, Isis turned toward him and offered a subtle nod, a silent confirmation that the coast was clear. She had settled into a comfortable chair she'd conjured on the rooftop, her gaze fixed on the glittering cityscape sprawled beneath them.

A thoughtful frown creased Rye's brow as he formulated his next message to Hal.

"It's regarding Set," he projected telepathically. "We need Damascus steel, specifically for spear tips. Ten would be ideal, mounted on wooden or steel poles. But here's the key – they need to be genuine Damascus steel from times gone by."

Understanding flickered in Hal's response.

"Yessir, Set is a volatile entity. With enough spears, I imagine you could keep him at bay. He's the biggest wild card in this whole situation."

A beat of silence followed, and then Hal continued.

"Yessir, acquiring true Damascus steel is well within our capabilities. Once we have them, the esteemed Horus can imbue them with the violet flame, transforming them into divine weapons."

Relief washed over Rye. Having these divinely-charged spears at their disposal would significantly tip the scales in their favor.

"My friend," he projected with sincerity. "Blessings to you and all of your kind. I appreciate your unwavering support. I'll take a break from our telepathic conversation for now."

A hint of amusement colored his next transmission.

"How good it feels to be back in touch with you, Hal. It's truly wonderful to hear from you again."

"Yessir, the sentiment is entirely mutual," Hal replied, his voice filled with genuine warmth. "Having you retrieved from such a long absence is remarkable. My entire group is elated to know you're back among us."

With a satisfied smile, Rye disconnected from the mental link. He pushed himself off the rooftop with a gentle burst of telekinetic energy, rising quickly into the air.

As he drifted, a sudden sensation tickled his nose. He blinked, startled, to find a tiny, shimmering creature hovering mere inches from his face. It was a pixie, no bigger than his thumb, with gossamer wings that shimmered with an otherworldly iridescence. Its pointed ears twitched, and its large, luminous eyes regarded him with an innocent curiosity.

"Who knew?" Rye breathed out, a mixture of surprise and amusement coloring his voice.

Isis' telepathic message echoed in his mind.

"Who knew such things lived on Earth?"

Rye chuckled softly.

"Who knew such things cared so much for Earth?" he projected back, a newfound sense of wonder blooming within him.

The universe, it seemed, was far more wondrous and diverse than he could have ever imagined.

Chapter 10

As the sun rose, Rye hovered above the roof, his legs slightly bent, spinning slowly in a gentle circle. His mind was awash with thoughts of Ena and Mal, their recent adventures still vivid in his memory.

He turned to Isis and said, "I'm going to go ahead and contact those two. Hopefully, we can meet them and then travel to Luxor. Memphis is up in the Nile Delta."

"That sounds wonderful," Isis replied in excitement at the prospect of their journey.

Rye closed his eyes, his focus sharpening as he prepared to send a thought construct to both Mal and Ena. He visualized their faces and the sound of their voices, and with a deep breath, he projected his thoughts outward.

Moments later, a response buzzed through his mind, clear and bright.

"The best news in centuries!" exclaimed Ena, her voice echoing in Rye's mind. "So thrilled for you. Here is our location; we are together," she added, sending a burst of coordinates directly to him.

As if a human heads-up display had sprung to life before his eyes, Rye saw the path to Ena and Mal materialize. It looked tangible, as though he could reach out and trace the route with his fingers.

"I just remembered my display. Thanks to you," Rye thought to himself, a smile tugging at the corner of his mouth.

"Oh yes," Ena's voice came through again, laced with laughter. "Very helpful. Glad you recovered it."

Looking over at Isis, who was watching him with a mixture of curiosity and anticipation, Rye nodded. They both knew it was time to travel. Instinctually, Rye activated his display, locking onto the coordinates Mal and Ena had provided. The destination was south, into what was once upper Egypt, out in the desert but near the life-giving waters of the Nile River.

"Ready?" Rye asked, turning to Isis.

"Yep, all ready, captain," Isis replied with a grin, her eyes sparkling with excitement.

Together, they hovered up over the hotel's roof, rising higher into the dawn sky. The two came together, their movements synchronized as if in a dance. Arcing gracefully up into the air, they made the turn and began heading south, their spirits lifted by the promise of reunion and adventure.

As they flew, Rye sent out a thought construct to his friends: "We are on our way to visit you, Isis and I."

"Splendid, we are honored to receive a goddess, oh and you," Mal laughed, his tone light and teasing.

"Glad I fit in somewhere with someone," Rye laughed back, his words tinged with humor. "We're sailing over the prairie and desert; it'll take a moment to get to you."

"We really look forward to it," said Mal with genuine anticipation.

Rye and Isis continued their journey, soaring over the Nile River, the majestic life-bringer. Despite being dammed and shut off at the delta near Mal and Ena's home, the river maintained its magical presence. They observed the bustling activity below—boats gliding across the water, docks bustling with workers, and fields stretching far into the horizon.

"So much advancement, population growth, yet still the Nile flows," Rye telepathed to Isis, in both awe and reflection.

The landscape gradually shifted from the lush riverbank to the vast, open desert, hiding countless stories of the past beneath its sands. The freedom of zipping along the desert, unencumbered, next to Isis was exhilarating; Rye couldn't help but give her a gentle squeeze as they flew.

"I see their home coming up," Rye announced, spotting a structure in the distance. "It resembles a compound."

"Great," replied Isis, peering down at the approaching site with interest.

"Let's pull up fairly high and take it all in," Rye suggested, eager to get a better view.

They ascended above the L-shaped fencing that marked the boundaries of the compound. Tucked into the shorter leg of the L, a desert buggy was cleverly hidden under a camouflaged cover, barely discernible from their elevated vantage point as Rye and Isis prepared to descend.

Rye spent some time with a truck he adored, inspecting every part of it— the engine, the wheels, and the underside. He was genuinely surprised and immensely grateful for the opportunity to drive it around the sands near Mal's compound, reveling in the joy of maneuvering through the desert landscape.

Ena stepped out of the house, waving enthusiastically, with Mal following close behind. The sight of them stirred a wave of nostalgia in Rye, memories of past adventures flooding his mind.

"Ahoy," bellowed Mal, booming with warmth. "Who might this be after all this time? My friend—many blessings."

They embraced tightly, the familiarity of the gesture comforting. "It looks like you've earned a few wrinkles along the way," Mal joked lightly.

"Leave him be," Ena chided gently, her smile bright and welcoming. "He looks precisely the way I remember him. We're so glad you're out, Rye; escaping was no small feat."

"Yes, for sure," Rye agreed, a serious note entering his voice. "But I managed to pick up some great friends along the way. Allow me to introduce you to Isis, the mother of magick, the healer, wearer of the sun disk, and cobra, known by many names."

"Many blessings to you both," Isis greeted them warmly. "I have seen you, and your lives make the gods smile. You are held in high regard and will continue to be so. You will find that many gods and goddesses are approachable and jovial, not mere wallflowers painted on the side. But always ready to throw in and help or share a laugh, a moment of joy. We find that life is meant to be cherished.

"We have a gift for you that we have been keeping for a long time," Ena revealed with excitement. She presented Rye with a folded black box containing a piece of meteorite, the same material used to forge the legendary Ka sword.

Rye instantly recognized the material. As he lifted it, time seemed to slow down, and so did Rye's movements.

***

That night, the second night, the heroes—Rye, Isis, Mal, and Ena—made their way to Taposiris Magna, an ancient ruins site in southern Alexandria that remained open 24 hours a day. Amidst the towering columns and crumbling stone, they were to meet with Ammit to settle the terms of the pitched battle.

Under the moonlit sky, they found Ammit, mostly hidden in the shadows, seated by a large wooden table illuminated only by a single tall candle flickering in the breeze. Her presence was dreary, her eyes reflecting a deep-seated disdain.

Without waiting for any formalities, she declared in a gravelly voice, "Rye will deploy no light vampires in the battle." Rye was prepared to agree, but only on the condition that she would not put any dark vampires into the fray.

At that moment, a dark vampire materialized at the end of the table, a sinister figure that growled deeply, licking his sharp teeth with blood-red gums. He stood tall, nearly seven feet, with ethereal black mist swirling around him. His appearance was stoic, yet there was a wildness in his hypnotic all-black eyes that could unsettle even the bravest soul.

"I loathe you and your kind," he hissed menacingly.

Rye, maintaining his composure, could tell this vampire was of the upper echelon—ancient and powerful.

"I have no fear of you," Rye responded calmly, his voice steady. "I forgive you."

The wisping dark vampire seemed almost taken aback by Rye's lack of fear and his offer of forgiveness.

"It is only a matter of time, isn't it?" the vampire retorted. "We will trap each light vampire and have our ways with them for... centuries. You will know the reality of my torture. The nightmares."

Suddenly, Set stood up, his grey, massive skin more pronounced under the dim light, making him an imposing, aggressive figure.

"I miss you, red, and your little ways," he told Isis, tinged with a blend of mockery and nostalgia.

"Still climbing uphill, Set? You know there might not be an end to that," Isis replied sharply in a tone cool and unwavering.

"Wonderful, wonderful," croaked Ammit, breaking the tension. "We are all nearly ready. Is there anything else you would ask?" Her gaze shifted to Rye, piercing and intense. Now, with her so close, Rye could smell her terrible, rotting stench—a foul scent that seemed to cling to the air. It was then that Rye noticed a twinkle from the watchers in the sky, a silent audience to their dark council.

"Tell me your target. That will complete this meeting," Rye demanded, his voice resolute.

"And I will tell you," she belched out, her voice echoing ominously through the ruins. "The Borg El Arab Airport— we will begin collecting. You can join us for a grand party and games! This battle is pitched!"

"I miss you, red, and your little ways," he told Isis with a blend of mockery and nostalgia.

"Still climbing uphill, Set? You know there might not be an end to that," Isis replied sharply in a tone cool and unwavering.

"Wonderful, wonderful," croaked Ammit, breaking the tension. "We are all nearly ready. Is there anything else you would ask?" Her gaze shifted to Rye, piercing and intense.

Now, with her so close, Rye could smell her terrible, rotting stench—a foul scent that seemed to cling to the air. It was then that Rye noticed a twinkle from the watchers in the sky, a silent audience to their dark council.

"Tell me your target. That will complete this meeting," Rye demanded.

"And I will tell you," she belched out, her voice echoing ominously through the ruins. "The Borg El Arab Airport—we will begin collecting. You can join us for a grand party and games! This battle is pitched!"

"Very well," Rye finally said, his voice firm. "We will see you at the Borg El Arab Airport. Prepare yourself, Ammit, for we will not stand idly by."

Chapter 11

Rye, Mal, Ena, and the Arcturian Star Beings gathered near the edge of the runway. The smell of burnt concrete and charred metal lingered in the air, remnants of the fierce combat they had endured.

Rye's eyes scanned the distance, the desert stretching out before them. He turned to Mal, who was nursing a minor cut on his arm, his wind powers still swirling subtly around him, lifting grains of sand into the air. Ena, her hands glowing softly as she healed a wounded Arcturian, wearily glanced up at Rye.

"We don't have much time," Rye said. "We need to move and unlock the full potential of the ka sword before they regroup."

Mal nodded, rolling his shoulders to ease the tension. "I can scout ahead and make sure the path is clear."

Ena finished her healing and stood up, brushing the sand off her hands. "I'll keep an eye on the rear. We don't want any surprises."

Rye took a deep breath and closed his eyes, focusing on the telepathic trail he could only sense. Soon, a glowing path began to materialize in his mind. He opened his eyes and pointed toward the west. "The trail leads that way. Stay close and stay alert."

As they set out, the landscape quickly transitioned from the cracked tarmac of the airport to the shifting sands of the desert. The sun hung low in the sky; each footstep seemed to pull them deeper into a world of endless sand and silence.

Mal moved to the front, his eyes sharp as he surveyed their surroundings. He extended his hand, summoning a gentle breeze that pushed back the encroaching heat. Ena walked beside him, her senses attuned to any sign of danger, while the Arcturian Star Beings flanked them, their presence both comforting and formidable.

The first few hours passed in a tense silence, broken only by the soft crunch of sand underfoot. Every now and then, Rye would close his eyes, recalibrating their direction as the telepathic trail shifted and twisted through the desert. The further they went, the stronger the connection became, pulling them inexorably toward their destination.

As the sun climbed higher, the heat became more oppressive. Sweat trickled down Rye's forehead, but the sunlight made him feel as if he possessed all power in the world, "We're getting closer," Rye said, "I can feel it."

Mal wiped his brow and took a swig from his water flask. "Good. Let's keep moving. We don't want to be caught out here when night falls."

Ena nodded in agreement, her eyes scanning the place for any sign of movement.

As they resumed their trek, the landscape began to change subtly. The dunes grew steeper, and the sand took on a darker hue. Rye could feel the telepathic trail pulsing with greater intensity, guiding them toward a specific point in the vast desert.

Suddenly, Mal held up a hand, signaling for them to stop. He crouched low, his eyes narrowing as he surveyed the area ahead, searching for any sign of disturbance. "Something's not right," he murmured. "I can feel a disturbance in the air."

Rye nodded to Ena. She moved forward cautiously, her light powers ready to defend against any threat.

As they moved forward, the sand beneath their feet began to shift unnaturally. The ground trembled, and a low rumble echoed through the desert. Rye felt a surge of dark energy, and his heart quickened. "Get ready," he warned. "We're not alone."

Without warning, the sand beneath a nearby dune shifted dramatically. It was not the gentle slide of sand dislodged by the wind but a violent upheaval, as if the earth itself was breaking open. From this rupture, dark figures emerged, coalescing from the sands into solid form with alarming speed.

These were the Death walkers, but not as they had encountered them before. These creatures bore the marks of deeper, darker enchantments. Their forms were more defined. Taller than a man, with limbs that twisted unnaturally and skin that shimmered like oil, their presence distorted the air around them. Eyes glowed crimson, and shadows clung to them like a shroud, twisting and writhing with malevolent life, and their mouths, lined with jagged teeth, hung agape in silent snarls.

The group halted, forming a circle back-to-back, each facing an outward direction. Mal acted first, his hands sweeping up as he called to the wind. A gust whipped around them, stirring the sand into a blinding storm. However, the Death walkers moved through it, their forms slicing through the swirling sands without hindrance.

Ena, her palms glowing, prepared to unleash her light. She waited, her focus on the shifting figures, timing her assault. As the first Deathwalker lunged forward, she thrust her hands out, beams of pure light shooting forth. The light hit its target, and for a moment, the creature recoiled, its form flickering under the assault. But it was a brief victory; the creature's resilience was formidable, quickly regathering its composure and pressing forward.

The battle grew desperate. Rye relied on his combat skills honed over many battles. He dodged and weaved through the attackers.

Mal, beside him, created barriers of wind that diverted the Death walkers but did not deter them. He shouted over the howl of the gale, "They're adapting to every move!"

Ena continued to send forth arcs of light, brightening the dark forms of their enemies. The light seared the Death walkers , slowing their advance and causing smoke to rise from their charred flesh. Yet, they kept coming.

The creatures regrouped, and it became apparent they were learning, adapting their tactics to counter the elemental forces besieging them. Their movements became more coordinated; they started to flank, surround, and drive the group tighter.

The sand beneath them shifted again, more violently this time. A massive Deathwalker emerged, larger than the others and radiating an aura of dark energy. It stood before Rye, towering over him, its eyes burning deep red. This was the embodiment of Ammit's will, a creature forged from the darkest magic of the desert.

Rye met its gaze, and the creature roared, a sound that vibrated through the very sand beneath their feet. It charged, its movements a blur of speed and power.

The clash was monumental. Rye ducked under a sweeping claw, rolled across the sand, and came up just as the creature barreled past. Seeing an opening, Mal directed a concentrated blast of wind at the creature's back, propelling it slightly off course. Seizing the moment, Ena focused her light into a single, piercing beam aimed directly at the creature's eyes. The Deathwalker stumbled, blinded momentarily, its arms flailing to regain balance.

The Deathwalker regained its footing, shaking off the disorientation with a guttural snarl that sent ripples through the air. It turned sharply, his steps now zeroed in on Rye again. The desert was now booming with the sounds of more emerging Death walkers .

The new wave was not like the ones before; they were taller, their limbs gnarled with the power of the dark magic that animated them. Their eyes did not just glow; they burned with a malevolence that seemed to suck the very light from the air. As they formed ranks, the atmosphere thickened, the natural magic of the desert recoiling from the perversion of its essence.

Mal positioned himself beside Rye. He spread his arms wide, palms facing the storm of sand kicked up by the enemy's advance. With a deep, inhaled breath, he summoned the wind. At first, a gentle breeze stirred the loose sand at their feet, but with Mal's focused intent, it grew rapidly into a howling gale.

Rye nodded, and with a thrust of his arm, he directed a stream of fire from his eyes, the flames catching the wind's draft and transforming into a swirling inferno that rushed toward the advancing Death walkers .

The firestorm took on a life of its own, fanned by Mal's tempest; it became a wall of flame that roared across the battlefield. The heat was intense, the light blinding, and the Death walkers halted their charge. The flames did not burn them as fire would flesh; instead, they disrupted the dark magic that held their forms together. Shadows within their bodies wavered, and for a moment, it seemed they might dissipate.

However, the creatures were resilient. They regrouped quickly. The Death walkers began to use more of the desert to their advantage, manipulating the sand to create swirling dust devils that attempted to blind and disorient the defenders. Rye, Mal, and Ena found themselves having to adapt rapidly to the multiplicity of tactics being employed against them.

In the middle of the desert's manipulated elements, Ena became the focal point of stability for her beleaguered group. Ena stepped forward in the storm and moved toward a subdued Deathwalker. As she reached the creature, her hand extended, and a soft but firm glow enveloped her palm. She touched the Deathwalker, and the effect was instantaneous. As her fingers brushed against the coarse, shadow-woven skin of the Deathwalker, a visible shudder ran through its frame. The dark magic, a force that had bound the creature's will, met the purifying energy radiated by Ena's touch. The effect was immediate.

The transformation was not merely physical. The creature's posture shifted; where there was once aggression, now there was calm, a stillness that spoke of freed will. Ena moved to the next Deathwalker, repeating the process. Each touch not only transformed but also visibly weakened the dark magic.

Ammit had woven into these beings. The more she converted, the more the tide of battle shifted, creating new allies from former enemies.

Around them, the battle raged on, but at that moment, a silent understanding passed between Ena and the newly freed being. Without a word, it stepped forward, positioning itself between Ena and an incoming attack, its actions now driven by a will to protect.

Seeing this, Rye and Mal paused momentarily in awe and, catching on, began to herd more of the subdued Death walkers toward Ena, using gusts of wind to gently guide them into her range. Each touch from Ena brought another ally to their side, each conversion weakening the enemy's numbers and bolstering their own.

The transformed Death walkers began to act with purpose. They used their intimate knowledge of their former brethren's tactics against them. They anticipated moves, countered attacks, and protected the trio of humans who had given them back their freedom. Their actions spoke louder than any words could; they fought not out of subservience but out of gratitude and newfound kinship.

As each Deathwalker was transformed, they turned to face their former allies, reaching out in a gesture that was both defensive and enlightening. They touched their comrades, attempting to pass on the liberation they had experienced. The chain reaction was slow but visible as pockets of resistance started to form within the ranks of the dark minions.

Rye, witnessing the growing number of allies, shouted encouragement, "Keep pushing! They're breaking!"

As the tide of battle turned, the sands settled, and the last of the enemy was either subdued or transformed, a quiet fell over the desert. Rye, Mal, and Ena stood surrounded by their new allies, no longer just a band of weary travelers. They had turned enemies into allies.

"How did you do it, Ena?" Mal asked, breathing heavily.

"Let's just say it's a little secret," she replied, giving him a smirk.

"Alright, you two. We have no time," Rye said to the two of them and then turned his attention to the Death walkers. "We move forward together," Rye declared, "This victory is not just ours but yours. You have regained your will and, with it, the choice to help us end this tyranny."

The newly transformed Death walkers , understanding their role in the battles to come, nodded in agreement, their eyes bright with the light of free will. Together, they set out deeper into the desert, toward the unknown challenges ahead, under the leadership of Rye.

Chapter 12

As the group, bolstered by their newly allied Death walkers , ventured deeper into the desert, the scorching sun began to set. The journey was silent except for the crunch of sand underfoot, bringing them closer to their destination: The ancient temple where the Ka sword was believed to be hidden.

Rye led the way. Beside him, Mal and Ena discussed their strategy in hushed tones, wary of what lay ahead.

The transformed Death walkers moved with an unnerving grace along with the group. It was as if the group was leading an army of its own. Their once menacing presence now added a layer of security for them. They communicated silently among themselves; their crimson eyes now had a gentle glow.

As they approached the coordinates that Rye's telepathic trail had revealed, the sands began to rise sharply, forming towering dunes that tested the endurance of the group. Climbing the steep slopes, they relied heavily on the Death walkers ' strength and knowledge of the terrain.

The sun had almost set when they reached the crest of the highest dune, and there, in a valley below, lay the ancient temple. It was a grand structure, its stone walls worn but still standing resilient against the desert's harshness. Intricate carvings adorned its facade, depicting scenes of ancient rituals and celestial alignments.

"Looks like we're here," Rye announced in relief.

The group descended into the valley, their eyes fixed on the massive doors of the temple. As they drew closer, a subtle vibration began to fill the air, a whisper of ancient magic that seemed to emanate from the very stones of the structure.

The Arcturian Star Beings, who had silently guarded their flanks during the journey, turned to Rye and said, "This might be where we part ways."

"Your wisdom has guided us well, but I can see that the path forward is meant for us alone," he replied.

The Arcturians, their features inscrutable, nodded in understanding. With a grace that spoke of their celestial origin, they each placed a hand upon the temple's walls, their touch leaving a faint glow that slowly spread across the carvings.

"We leave a part of our essence to aid you," they intoned, their voices like a melody fading into the wind. "May it light your way in the darkness."

With that, they turned and disappeared into the desert, their forms gradually fading until they were nothing more than a whisper on the wind.

Turning back to the temple, Rye approached the massive doors. They were carved with depictions of the Ka sword. He reached out, placing his hand on the door, and the carvings began to glow with a golden light. The doors trembled and then slowly opened, revealing a dark passage that led into the heart of the temple.

The group entered cautiously, walking into the empty hallways. The air inside was cool and smelled of sandalwood and myrrh. Torches flared to life along the walls as they passed, illuminating wall hangings and murals that told the history of the Ka sword and its keepers.

Their path led them deeper into the temple through chambers filled with ancient artifacts and dusty tomes. The walls here were lined with hieroglyphs that Ena attempted to decipher, her fingers tracing the outlines of symbols that spoke of balance, power, and destiny.

As the group reached a giant chamber, they saw three towering figures standing there, each cloaked in robes, with faces obscured by masks of gold, silver, and obsidian.

"Who dares seek the power of the Ka swords in the sacred sanctum of the ancients?" The figure in gold stepped forward and said as if it had sensed what Rye was here for.

Rye stepped forward, "We are seekers of balance and defenders against tyranny. We come to claim the power to protect our world."

The silver figure moved gracefully, almost floating toward them. "Words are but air. We must test your worth through trials. Only those of true heart can wield the power hidden within these walls."

The obsidian figure raised its arms, and the ground beneath them trembled. "Prepare for the first trial. You must demonstrate your balance, not just of mind, but of force and spirit."

The chamber's floor shifted, transforming into a massive grid of tiles, each glowing faintly. The golden figure explained, "Each tile represents a virtue or vice. Step correctly and advance. Err, and face the consequences. Your entire group must cross to succeed."

Mal whispered to the group, keeping his eyes on the shifting tiles, "We need to support each other. Watch the patterns and keep a balance."

Rye nodded, taking the lead. He stepped forward onto a tile that glowed with a soft blue light, feeling a calm assurance flood through him. As each member of their group took a step, some tiles glowed warmly, reinforcing their choice, while others flickered ominously, nearly throwing them off balance with bursts of unsettling energy.

Ena, focusing her senses, reached out to feel the energies of the tiles ahead. "The tiles react to our intentions. We must align our actions with virtues: courage, humility, compassion."

As they progressed, the patterns became more complex. Mal faced a moment of doubt as he reached a crossroads of tiles. Glancing back at Rye and Ena, he took a deep breath and chose a path illuminated by a gentle golden hue, representing courage. The tile solidified under his feet, supporting his choice.

The transformed Death walkers , uncertain at first, began to understand the significance of their actions. They moved cautiously, learning from the group and adapting to the trial's demands.

Just as they were nearing the end of the grid, a large tile was in front. Rye turned to Ena, seeking guidance. She studied the area, then pointed to a less conspicuous tile to the left, bathed in a soft white light. "Humility, Rye. It's the safer path."

He nodded, stepping onto the white tile. It held firm, and a sense of peace reassured him. With one last collective effort, they reached the other side of the chamber, where the golden figure awaited.

"Well done," it said, the voice now softer, approving. "You have demonstrated balance in your steps and decisions. Prepare for the next trial, which will test your unity and individual strengths."

The group took a moment to regroup, sharing glances of relief. They had passed the first test but knew the challenges ahead would only grow more demanding.

As they braced themselves, the silver figure gestured to a doorway that glowed with a pulsating light, signaling the beginning of the next challenge.

The doorway led them into a circular arena surrounded by towering statues of the ancient gods. The silver figure followed them in, its robe flickering like moonlight against the dark walls.

"This trial," it began, "will test your unity and individual strength. You must defeat the guardians crafted from the very essence of this temple. They are not mere constructs; they will adapt and learn from your tactics."

As the echo of its voice faded, the statues around the arena stirred to life, their stone surfaces cracking to reveal bodies of shimmering crystal. These guardians moved with surprising agility, their forms blurring in swift, calculated motions.

Rye was glancing at Mal and Ena. "We need to work together. Each guardian is different. We adapt, we support each other, and we stay aware."

Mal nodded, his eyes focusing on the nearest guardian. It was a towering figure wielding a crystal spear that seemed to absorb the faint light within the arena. "I'll take the lead on this one," he declared, stepping forward with a surge of wind gathering at his fingertips.

As Mal engaged the first guardian, directing gusts of wind to unbalance it, Rye and Ena focused on another that approached from the side, its arms morphing into shields as it advanced. Rye met it head-on with a stone sword he had found in the temple, clashing against the crystalline shield, sparks illuminating the darkened arena.

Meanwhile, Ena extended her hands, her palms glowing with intense light. She focused her energy, sending beams toward the joints of the guardian's shields, looking for weak spots in its seemingly impenetrable defense.

The transformed Death walkers were not idle. Understanding the stakes, they paired up, using their enhanced strength and newfound tactics to outmaneuver a third guardian that had joined the fray. Their movements were synchronized, a dance of shadows and light as they alternated attacks to keep the guardian off balance.

"Keep a balance between attack and defense!" Rye called out, ducking under a sweeping blow from his guardian. He pivoted, slashing upwards, finding a crack in the guardian's armor. The crystal shuddered under the impact, a web of fractures spreading from the point of contact.

Mal, observing the effectiveness of Rye's strike, adapted his approach. He concentrated the wind into a sharp, focused burst, aiming at the legs of his guardian. The force was enough to knock the guardian off its feet, giving Mal a crucial opening to strike at its core.

As each guardian fell, they dissolved into the ground, their essence seeping back into the stone of the arena. With each victory, the group's confidence grew, but so did their exhaustion. The trial was a test of endurance as much as strength and unity.

After the last guardian collapsed into shimmering dust, the silver figure reappeared, nodding in approval. "You have shown great unity and adaptability. Your strengths complement one another, and your resolve is clear."

Exhausted but undeterred, the group gathered in the center of the arena, catching their breath and preparing for the final trial. The silver figure pointed toward another archway, this one radiating a soft, green light.

"The final trial awaits," it said. "It will test your wisdom and your ability to foresee the consequences of your choices. Proceed when you are ready."

With a collective nod, they moved toward the archway, stepping into the light that would lead them to the final challenge.

As the group stepped through the archway into the third and final chamber, they found themselves in a vast, echoing hall. The ceiling soared high above, decorated with intricate mosaics that depicted ancient battles, celestial alignments, and the cycles of nature. The light in this room was dim, suffused with a soft green glow.

The obsidian figure materialized before them. "This trial," it intoned, "is not one of physical strength nor of mere cunning. It will test your wisdom, your ability to foresee consequences, and your capacity to act with foresight and understanding."

As the figure spoke, the floor of the chamber shifted, revealing a complex maze of paths branching out in multiple directions. Each path was lined with doors, their surfaces inscribed with cryptic symbols and phrases. Above each door was an inscription, offering a vague clue as to the nature of the challenge behind it.

Rye examined the inscriptions with a keen eye. "We need to think ahead," he said, his voice steady but serious. "These doors aren't just about what lies behind them."

Ena moved beside him, her fingers gently tracing the symbols etched into the nearest door. "This one reads, 'Through the fire, the spirit is tested.' It suggests a challenge of endurance, but we must consider what we could lose if we take this path."

Mal approached another door, studying the inscription: "Shadows lengthen as the light fades." He turned to the group. "This could be a trial of deception or confronting inner darkness. It's about what it does to us."

Rye looked to the transformed Death walkers , who had become invaluable allies. "Your insight could be crucial here. What do your instincts tell you?"

One of the Death walkers , a figure who had once been a creature of darkness, stepped forward. "We know the path of shadows well. It is fraught with deception and the temptation to revert to old ways. But it also offers the chance to confront and overcome our past."

Considering their options carefully, the group decided to split into three teams, each tackling a different path to maximize their chances of success and to gain a broader understanding of the temple's trials.

Rye, along with two of the Death walkers , chose the path of fire. They passed through the door, and immediately, the temperature rose. The corridor they entered was narrow, the walls glowing with an intense heat. Flames flickered along the edges, threatening to engulf them at any moment.

Rye felt exposed, but he knew he had to rely on his wits and the strength of his companions. "Stay close," he instructed, "We need to move quickly but carefully."

The heat grew more oppressive as they advanced. The path narrowed further, forcing them to maneuver carefully to avoid the licking flames. At one point, the flames surged, blocking their way completely.

One of the Death walkers , sensing the danger, stepped forward. It raised its arms and, with a deep, resonant chant, began to draw the flames toward itself, absorbing the heat and fire into its own form. The other Deathwalker joined in, their combined efforts creating a temporary barrier that allowed Rye to pass through safely.

"Are you sure you can hold this?" Rye asked, concerned.

The first Deathwalker nodded, "We were forged in darkness and fire. This is a trial we can endure."

Rye hurried through the flames, reaching the end of the corridor where a lever jutted out from the wall. He pulled it with all his strength, and the flames suddenly subsided, leaving the corridor cool and dark once more.

The Death walkers , now visibly drained, followed Rye to the end of the path. "You did well," Rye said, placing a hand on their shoulders. "We wouldn't have made it without you."

Meanwhile, Ena led her group through the door inscribed with the phrase, "Where waters run deep, wisdom prevails." They stepped into a chamber filled with a tranquil pool of water, the surface so still that it reflected the ceiling above perfectly, creating the illusion of endless depth.

Ena approached the edge of the pool cautiously. "This trial is about understanding, about seeing beyond the surface," she mused. "There's more here than meets the eye."

She knelt by the water, peering into its depths. Her reflection stared back at her, but something was off. The reflection's eyes were filled with uncertainty and doubt that Ena knew she had long overcome. "This water shows us our inner conflicts, our unresolved fears."

The Death walkers beside her knelt as well, their reflections revealing their past selves: dark, twisted forms that they had struggled to break free from. One of them, clearly disturbed by the vision, stepped back, nearly losing balance.

Ena reached out, steadying the Deathwalker. "These reflections are not our reality. They are what we might become if we let our fears rule us."

The trial required them to navigate the pool, but the water was not as shallow as it seemed. As they began to wade through, the reflections shifted, showing different futures: somewhere they succeeded, others where they failed disastrously. The water, once calm, began to churn with unseen currents, pulling them in different directions.

"Stay focused!" Ena shouted, fighting against the current. "We choose our own paths, not these illusions!"

With great effort, they reached the other side of the pool, the water stilling once more as they emerged, soaked but resolute. Ena's wisdom and the group's collective strength had carried them through the trial, dispelling the illusions and affirming their true selves.

Mal and the remaining Death walkers entered the door marked by the inscription, "Shadows lengthen as the light fades." The room they entered was filled with shifting shadows, the light flickering as if struggling to stay alive.

The shadows here were more than a mere absence of light; they were living entities, twisting and morphing into shapes that taunted and terrorized. Each step forward seemed to summon new forms, ghostly apparitions of past failures, fears, and doubts.

Mal took a deep breath, centering himself. "These shadows are here to deceive us, to make us question ourselves. We need to stand firm in who we are."

The shadows grew bolder as they advanced, their whispers becoming more insidious. They showed Mal visions of past mistakes, times when he had failed to protect those he cared about when his powers had not been enough. But Mal refused to be swayed.

"No more lies!" he shouted, summoning a gust of wind that blew the shadows back. "I know who I am, and I will not be bound by these fears!"

The Death walkers , drawing strength from Mal, began to fight back against the shadows. They used their own darkness, not to succumb but to absorb and transform the shadows, turning them into harmless wisps of smoke.

Together, they made their way through the room, dispelling the last of the shadows as they reached the end. Mal, though weary, felt pride in what they had accomplished. "We faced the darkness, and we overcame it. This was a victory of the spirit."

As each group completed their trials, they found themselves once again in the central chamber. The obsidian figure, now less imposing, watched them with a look of approval.

"You have all faced your trials with wisdom, courage, and unity," it said. "You have proven yourselves worthy of the power you seek."

The chamber's walls began to glow, and the maze of paths slowly faded, leaving behind a single, radiant door. This door led to the final prize, the culmination of their journey.

Rye, Mal, Ena, and the transformed Death walkers stood before it, their trials behind them. They had been tested in every way possible: physically, mentally, and emotionally and had emerged stronger for it.

The figures made way for them, and a massive door swung open. A rush of cool, ancient air greeted them. The light from the chamber beyond was soft, golden, and welcoming, unlike the trials they had just endured. The obsidian figure remained behind as the group stepped forward, offering a final, solemn nod of approval before fading into the shadows.

The chamber's walls were lined with intricate carvings and runes that pulsed with a faint, rhythmic light. At the center of the chamber, on a raised pedestal, rested the Ka sword. The blade was sheathed in an aura of shimmering energy, its surface reflecting the golden light that filled the room.

Rye felt a deep, almost magnetic pull toward the sword. He could sense its immense power but also the danger that surrounded it. The air crackled with energy, and he knew that retrieving the sword would not be as simple as reaching out and taking it.

"This is it," Rye said quietly, "The Ka sword."

Mal and Ena stepped closer, their eyes fixed on the blade. "Be careful, Rye," Ena warned him. "There's more here than meets the eye. The energy in this room… it's like it's alive."

Rye nodded, taking a deep breath as he approached the pedestal. "I can feel it, too. The sword is surrounded by ancient defenses. If we're not careful, we could trigger something that we can't control."

Mal studied the runes on the walls, his mind racing. "These markings… they seem to suggest a balance of forces. Light and dark, life and death. It's as if the sword is the key to maintaining that balance."

Rye, being a light vampire, could feel the light in the chamber nourishing him, energizing him. But he also sensed the darkness lurking at the edges, a counterbalance to the light that kept the forces in equilibrium. "If we want to retrieve the sword safely, I need to find a way to connect with both the light and the darkness here. They're two sides of the same coin, and if I can harmonize with both, we might avoid setting off any traps."

Ena looked at Rye, her eyes filled with trust. "You can do this, Rye. Just remember, keep a balance. Don't let one side overpower the other."

Rye closed his eyes, centering himself. He focused first on the light, drawing it into himself, feeling it fill him with warmth and power. The light was familiar and comforting, and it responded to him readily, flowing into him like a river of energy. His skin tingled as the light fed him, giving him strength.

But Rye knew that wasn't enough. He had to balance this with the darkness that lurked in the chamber. Tentatively, he reached out with his senses, touching the shadows that clung to the corners of the room. The darkness was cold and elusive, and for a moment, it recoiled from his light. But Rye persisted, letting the light within him dim just enough to allow the darkness to approach.

As the darkness began to mix with the light inside him, Rye felt a strange sensation. The two forces didn't clash; instead, they began to swirl together, like the mingling of night and day at dawn. It was a delicate balance, one that required all of Rye's focus to maintain. Too much light and the darkness would retreat, disrupting the harmony. Too much darkness and the light would be overwhelmed.

Mal and Ena watched as Rye's body began to glow with soft light, his eyes closed in deep concentration. The transformed Death walkers , sensing the delicate operation underway, stood silently, their eyes reflecting the shifting energies in the chamber.

Finally, Rye opened his eyes, which now glowed with a mixture of light and dark energy. He stepped forward, reaching out toward the Ka sword. As his hand drew closer, the energy surrounding the sword began to shift, reacting to the balance that Rye had achieved within himself.

"Careful…" Mal whispered.

Rye's hand hovered over the hilt of the sword. He could feel the ancient magic testing him, probing his balance of light and dark. But he held steady, refusing to let either side dominate. With a deep breath, he closed the final distance, wrapping his fingers around the hilt.

For a moment, the chamber was silent as if holding its breath. Then, the energy surrounding the sword flared, enveloping Rye in a cocoon of light and shadow. The runes on the walls pulsed with a blinding intensity before gradually dimming, settling into a steady glow.

Rye stood there, the Ka sword in his hand, unharmed. The ancient traps had been disarmed, their power neutralized by the balance he had achieved.

He turned to face his companions, the sword held firmly in his grip. "We did it," Rye said, "The sword is ours."

Chapter 13

As Rye, Mal, Ena, and the transformed Death walkers exited the temple, the cool night air swept over them. The group was buoyed by their success in retrieving the Ka sword. The sky above was clear, the stars twinkling like distant beacons, offering a brief moment of peace after the grueling trials.

But the tranquility of the night was shattered by a sudden, violent gust of wind that knocked them off balance. Rye immediately sensed something was wrong. The air carried a scent that was all too familiar—metallic, sharp, and laced with malice.

"Get ready!" Rye shouted, instinctively raising the Ka sword in a defensive stance. The transformed Death walkers flanked him, their eyes scanning the shadows for any signs of movement.

From the darkness, a figure emerged, tall and imposing, with eyes that burned a deep, hateful red. It was Shezmu, the ancient enforcer of chaos and destruction. His presence was suffocating, as if the very air around him was being drawn into a vortex of malevolence. His skin shimmered with a strange, oily sheen, reflecting the starlight in unsettling patterns.

"Did you think retrieving the sword would be the end?" Shezmu taunted, his voice like gravel grinding against steel.

"This temple holds more than just relics—it holds the power of judgment, and I am its executor."

Without warning, Shezmu launched himself at the group, moving with a speed that belied his size. Rye barely had time to react as Shezmu's first strike landed, the force of the blow sending him skidding back. The impact reverberated through Rye's arm, and he tightened his grip on the Ka sword, channeling his light energy to steady himself.

Mal quickly summoned a gust of wind, aiming to knock Shezmu off balance, but Shezmu barely flinched. He seemed to absorb the force of the wind, using it to fuel his own momentum as he advanced. Ena threw a beam of concentrated light, but Shezmu deflected it effortlessly, his dark aura absorbing the attack as if it were nothing more than a faint breeze.

"Spread out!" Rye ordered, realizing that their usual tactics were ineffective. "He's adapting too quickly!"

The group fanned out, trying to surround Shezmu, but the ancient enforcer was relentless. He moved like a storm, his attacks coming from all angles, each strike carrying the weight of centuries of darkness. The transformed Death walkers tried to intercept, their forms now fully attuned to the light, but Shezmu swatted them away with terrifying ease, his strength overpowering their combined efforts.

Rye darted forward, slashing with the Ka sword, aiming for a critical strike. But Shezmu caught the blade with his bare hand, the metal screeching as his grip tightened. Rye's eyes widened in shock as Shezmu grinned, his teeth sharp and glinting.

"You think you can wield the power of balance against me?" Shezmu sneered, pushing the sword back with such force that Rye was thrown off his feet. "You are playing with forces beyond your comprehension!"

Mal and Ena rushed to Rye's side, helping him back up. Mal's winds circled them protectively while Ena tried to buy them time with bursts of light, but Shezmu continued his onslaught, unrelenting and seemingly invulnerable.

"We need a new plan!" Mal shouted, his voice strained as he struggled to maintain their defenses.

Rye's mind raced. They couldn't outmatch Shezmu in raw power; that much was clear. But the temple itself was ancient, filled with traps and mechanisms designed to protect its secrets. If they could lure Shezmu inside, they might stand a chance.

"We have to get back into the temple," Rye said, panting from the effort of fending off Shezmu's attacks. "We can use the corridors to our advantage—make him fight on our terms."

Ena nodded, understanding immediately. "The temple's layout is intricate. We can use it to set traps, slow him down."

Rye turned to the transformed Death walkers , who had regrouped despite their injuries. "Can you create barriers and distractions? Anything to keep him off us while we move?"

One of the Death walkers , its eyes burning with determination, stepped forward. "We will hold him as long as we can. Go!"

With a nod, the group began a tactical retreat back toward the temple entrance. Shezmu, sensing their intent, roared in anger and lunged forward, but the Death walkers sprang into action, their forms glowing brightly as they erected barriers of light to block his path. Shezmu smashed through them with brute force, but each barrier slowed his advance, giving the group precious seconds to make it to the safety of the temple's corridors.

Once inside, Rye led them deeper, weaving through the narrow passageways. The walls echoed with the sounds of Shezmu's rage as he pursued them, his roars shaking the very foundation of the temple.

"We need to get to the chamber with the shifting tiles," Rye said, his voice urgent. "It's a natural choke point. We can use it to trap him."

Mal and Ena nodded, keeping pace as they navigated the maze-like halls. Behind them, the Death walkers continued their valiant efforts, using every ounce of their remaining strength to slow Shezmu's relentless pursuit.

They reached the chamber with the shifting tiles, its floor still glowing faintly from their earlier trial. Rye quickly scanned the room, his mind calculating the best way to use the environment to their advantage.

"If we can lure him onto the wrong tiles, we might be able to trap him in a cycle," Ena suggested, her eyes darting between the symbols on the floor.

Mal positioned himself by the entrance, ready to use his wind powers to steer Shezmu where they needed him. "Let's hope he's as reckless as he looks."

The plan was set, but they knew they had only moments before Shezmu would break through. The air was thick with tension, every second feeling like an eternity as they prepared for the enforcer's arrival.

The ground shook as Shezmu barreled into the chamber, his eyes blazing with fury. He paused briefly, scanning the room, a flicker of recognition in his gaze as he saw the shifting tiles. But his anger overwhelmed any caution; with a snarl, he charged forward straight into their trap.

"Now!" Rye yelled.

Mal unleashed a powerful gust, directing Shezmu toward a tile marked with a dark symbol. The enforcer stumbled slightly but kept coming, his focus singularly on Rye. Ena, standing at the far end of the chamber, used her light powers to create a blinding flash, forcing Shezmu to step back—right onto another dangerous tile.

The floor shifted beneath Shezmu, the tiles reacting to his missteps. Stone spikes shot up from the ground, narrowly missing him as he dodged to the side, only to trigger another trap. Shezmu roared in frustration, his movements becoming erratic as he struggled to maintain his balance.

Rye seized the moment, rushing in with the Ka sword. Though he couldn't overpower Shezmu directly, he used precise, calculated strikes, aiming for the weak points revealed by the shifting tiles. The enforcer staggered, caught between the traps and Rye's relentless attacks.

For the first time, Shezmu appeared vulnerable, his defenses cracking under the pressure of the temple's mechanisms. But Rye knew they couldn't let up—not yet.

"Keep him off balance!" Rye shouted, his voice cutting through the chaos. "We're almost there!"

With every step, Shezmu was drawn further into the trap, his once-unstoppable advance now a desperate struggle against the very environment he had underestimated. The battle was far from over, but for the first time, Rye and his allies had the upper hand.

They just had to keep it.

The stone walls of the temple trembled as Shezmu's relentless assault continued. Rye, Mal, and Ena worked frantically, their eyes darting between the ancient carvings and the mechanisms embedded in the temple walls. The Death walkers , despite their injuries and exhaustion, stood firm at the entrance to the chamber where Shezmu was trapped, their glowing forms bracing against the onslaught.

"Almost there," Mal muttered, his hands deftly manipulating the levers and switches. The ancient machinery groaned to life, gears turning and chains rattling as the temple's defenses began to activate.

Ena traced her fingers along a series of runes, her light powers illuminating the symbols as she deciphered the instructions. "These controls can channel the temple's energy," she said, her voice tinged with urgency. "If we do this right, we can direct it all at Shezmu. But it's a one-shot deal. If we miss—"

"We won't miss," Rye interrupted, his gaze focused and intense. "We'll lure him into position and hit him with everything we've got."

The temple shuddered again as Shezmu's blows grew more violent, the cracks in the stone doors widening. The Death walkers , now fully committed, channeled their own light and dark energies into the barriers, buying the group precious seconds. But Rye could see the strain in their eyes; they were reaching their limits.

"We have to move fast," Rye said, stepping back from the controls. "Mal, you and Ena keep the mechanism ready. I'll draw Shezmu into position."

Mal nodded, his expression grim but resolute. "We'll be ready. Just give us the signal."

Rye turned to the Death walkers . "Hold him off for just a little longer. As soon as I give the word, fall back."

The lead Deathwalker, its form flickering with the effort of maintaining the barrier, nodded. "We will not falter."

With a deep breath, Rye moved to the center of the chamber, positioning himself directly in front of the massive stone doors. He could feel the energy of the temple thrumming through the floor, a subtle vibration that resonated with the Ka sword in his grasp. He knew that this was their last chance to turn the tide.

"Ready?" Rye called back, his eyes fixed on the weakening doors.

"Ready," Mal and Ena confirmed in unison, their hands poised over the controls.

The doors finally gave way with a deafening crack, and Shezmu burst through, his form wreathed in a dark, swirling aura. His eyes blazed with fury as he spotted Rye standing alone in the center of the chamber. With a roar, Shezmu charged his movements a blur of speed and power.

Rye stood his ground, the Ka sword glowing faintly as he channeled his own light energy into the blade. He knew he couldn't overpower Shezmu directly, but he didn't need to. All he had to do was hold Shezmu's attention long enough to get him into the trap.

Shezmu closed the distance in an instant, swinging a massive fist at Rye. Rye ducked under the blow, rolling to the side as the impact shattered the stone floor where he had been standing. He retaliated with a quick slash of the Ka sword, the blade sparking against Shezmu's arm but failing to penetrate the enforcer's thick, armored skin.

"You think you can challenge me with that toy?" Shezmu snarled, swiping at Rye with his other hand. Rye dodged again, keeping Shezmu moving, keeping him focused.

"Now!" Rye shouted, diving to the side as Shezmu lunged forward.

Mal and Ena slammed their hands down on the controls. The ancient mechanisms roared to life, and the floor beneath Shezmu erupted with a blinding light. The chamber was filled with a deafening hum as the temple's energy coalesced, beams of light shooting out from the walls and ceiling, converging on Shezmu's position.

Shezmu roared in defiance, his dark aura flaring as he tried to absorb the energy. But the concentrated blast was too much, even for him. The light seared through his defenses, piercing his armor and striking at his very core. For the first time, Shezmu staggered, his movements slowing as the combined forces of the temple and the Ka sword overwhelmed him.

Rye didn't hesitate. With Shezmu momentarily stunned, he charged forward, the Ka sword blazing with a brilliant light. He aimed for the gaps in Shezmu's armor, thrusting the blade with all his strength. The sword struck true, sinking deep into Shezmu's chest. The enforcer let out a choked gasp, his red eyes widening in shock.

Rye twisted the blade, and a surge of energy erupted from the point of contact, blasting Shezmu backward. He crashed against the chamber wall, his form flickering as the darkness around him dissipated. The temple's light continued to pour into him, relentless and purifying, until Shezmu's once-mighty form crumbled into a pile of ash and smoke.

For a long moment, the chamber was silent. The light gradually faded, and the mechanisms powered down, leaving only the faint glow of the runes on the walls. Rye stood panting; the Ka sword still clutched in his hand, its energy spent but victorious.

Mal and Ena approached cautiously, their eyes fixed on the spot where Shezmu had fallen. "Is it over?" Mal asked, his voice hushed, as if afraid to break the fragile quiet.

Rye nodded, his shoulders sagging with exhaustion. "It's over."

Ena let out a breath of relief, her hand resting on Rye's shoulder. "You did it, Rye. You balanced the light and the dark. We all did."

The transformed Death walkers gathered around, their expressions a mix of triumph and fatigue. They had stood against Shezmu, fought alongside Rye and his companions, and together, they had emerged victorious.

"Thank you," Rye said to the Death walkers , his voice filled with gratitude. "We couldn't have done this without you."

The lead Deathwalker inclined its head. "We fought for our freedom and for the light you showed us. We will continue to fight for as long as we are needed."

Rye nodded, a sense of respect passing between them. They had faced Shezmu and won, but the journey was far from over. There were still battles to be fought, still darkness to be confronted. But with the Ka sword in hand and allies by their side, Rye knew they would face whatever came next with courage and determination.

As the group made their way out of the temple, the first rays of dawn broke over the horizon, bathing the desert in a warm, golden light. It was a new day, a new beginning, and for the first time in a long while, Rye felt a glimmer of hope for the future.

They had won this battle, but the war for balance had only just begun.

Chapter 14

Rye and his team barely had a moment to catch their breath after the battle with Shezmu when the ground beneath them began to tremble. The sand shifted violently, spiraling and pulling everything toward a single point in front of the temple. In seconds, the desert transformed into a massive sand funnel, spinning with a force that sucked in debris, rocks, and even the remnants of ancient structures that dotted the landscape. The sky above them darkened as if Ammit's presence had blotted out the sun.

Ammit emerged at the center of the vortex, her form towering and distorted, a grotesque embodiment of chaos and vengeance. She hovered above the funnel's core, her eyes blazing with a power that warped reality around her. Her very presence seemed to tear at the fabric of the world, creating ripples of distortion that made it hard for Rye and his allies to maintain their footing.

"We can't keep this up if she keeps drawing power from the funnel!" Mal shouted over the howling winds. Sand whipped around them, stinging their faces and making it difficult to see.

Ena squinted through the storm, her light powers flickering as she tried to shield them from the worst of the chaos. "She's feeding off the energy of the grid! It's making her stronger by the second."

Rye's mind raced, piecing together the puzzle. The grid wasn't just a map of the temple's defenses; it was a conduit of power, one that Ammit was exploiting to fuel her ascent. He glanced at the Ka sword, its blade still glowing faintly from the energy of their last battle. If they could use the grid's energy to their advantage, they might have a chance to turn the tide.

"We need to get closer!" Rye called out, gripping the sword tightly. "If I can tap into the grid, we can redirect its power away from her!"

But getting closer was easier said than done. The funnel's pull was immense, and every step forward felt like pushing against a tidal wave. The ground shifted unpredictably beneath them, and more than once, Rye found himself slipping, only to catch himself at the last moment.

Ammit laughed, a sound that echoed through the swirling sands like the rumble of thunder. "You think you can stop me? I am chaos incarnate! The more you struggle, the more power I gain!"

With a sudden, sweeping motion, Ammit unleashed a blast of raw energy that tore through the sandstorm, aiming directly at Rye. He raised the Ka sword just in time, the blade absorbing the impact but sending a jolt of power through his entire body. He gritted his teeth, holding his ground as the force threatened to push him back.

"We're running out of time," Ena warned with urgency. "She's going to overpower us if we don't do something now!"

Rye nodded. They were in the heart of the storm, and there was no turning back. If they were going to defeat Ammit, they would have to face her head-on, using every ounce of strength they had left.

As they pressed forward, the funnel's core loomed ahead, a swirling maelstrom of sand and energy that seemed to stretch endlessly downwards. Rye knew that this was their only shot. He glanced at Mal and Ena, who nodded back, their expressions set in determination. They were ready to follow him into the storm, no matter the cost.

Together, they pushed toward the center. The wind roared around them, and the sand felt like needles against their skin. But they kept going, driven by the knowledge that this was their only chance to stop Ammit before her power became unstoppable.

Just as they reached the core, Rye felt the ground give way beneath him. The sand shifted, and he was pulled under, the funnel swallowing him whole. For a moment, everything was chaos, a blur of motion, heat, and blinding light. He struggled to orient himself, but the pressure was overwhelming, pressing against him from all sides.

Then, in the midst of the maelstrom, something changed. The heat intensified, burning away the layers of his skin, stripping him down to his very essence. It was excruciating, and Rye could feel every nerve screaming in protest. But beneath the pain, there was something else: a sense of release, of transformation. He was no longer just Rye, the warrior with a mission. He was becoming something more, something that transcended his former self.

The sand around him began to glow, and Rye realized that he was drawing energy from the funnel, just as Ammit had. But unlike her, he wasn't feeding on chaos. He was harmonizing with it, finding a balance between the light and darkness that swirled within him. His body, now stripped of all its former trappings, glowed with ethereal light, and he could feel the power of the Ka sword resonating with his own spirit.

As Rye rose from the depths of the funnel, his appearance had changed. His skin was gone, leaving only a thin film that revealed the muscles, bones, and organs beneath. He was clad in red pants and gold boots, a striking contrast against the swirling sands. His transformation was complete, and with it came a new understanding of his role in this battle.

He looked up to see Ammit hovering above, her expression shifting from triumph to confusion as she took in his new form. For the first time, she hesitated, sensing that something had fundamentally changed.

"Rye!" Mal shouted over the deafening roar of the funnel. "You look—"

"Different," Ena finished, her eyes wide as she took in Rye's altered appearance. Despite the shock, there was no time for questions. Ammit's power continued to surge, and they needed to act quickly.

Rye, sensing the shift in Ammit's demeanor, seized the opportunity. He raised the Ka sword, the meteorite blade shimmering with a mixture of light and darkness. He could feel the energy coursing through him, a balance that allowed him to stand against Ammit's overwhelming power. But just as he prepared to launch his attack, a searing pain shot through his side.

He stumbled, his vision blurring for a moment as the source of the attack came into view. One of the transformed Death walkers , its eyes now glowing with a sinister red hue, stood with a spear aimed directly at Rye. The betrayal hit like a physical blow, not just to his body but to his resolve. This wasn't just any Deathwalker; it was one of their own, corrupted by Ammit's influence and turned against them.

"Rye!" Mal's voice cut through the chaos as he rushed forward, using his wind powers to create a barrier between Rye and the rogue Deathwalker. "What the hell is going on?"

The Deathwalker snarled, its voice a twisted echo of what it once was, "You thought you could control us, bind us to your cause. But chaos is our true nature, and Ammit is our queen!"

Ammit's laughter rang out, sharp and mocking. "Did you really think you could win so easily, Rye? Chaos cannot be tamed, not even by someone like you."

Rye gritted his teeth, pushing himself to his feet. The betrayal stung, but he couldn't afford to let it shake his focus. He looked at the rogue Deathwalker, seeing the flickers of darkness that had taken root. It was clear that Ammit's power extended beyond mere physical strength. She was capable of corrupting even the strongest of wills.

"We need to neutralize it!" Ena shouted, sending a blast of light toward the Deathwalker. The corrupted entity dodged with unnatural speed, retaliating with a strike that sent a shockwave through the sand.

Rye raised the Ka sword, channeling the balance of light and dark within him. He focused on the Deathwalker, seeking not just to destroy but to sever the bond of corruption that Ammit had established. The blade glowed brighter, its energy resonating with Rye's intent.

As the Deathwalker lunged, Rye swung the Ka sword, the blade connecting with the creature's weapon. Sparks flew, and for a moment, the Deathwalker's form flickered as if caught between its corrupted state and its true self. Rye pushed harder, drawing on the energy of the sword to cut through the darkness that had taken hold.

With a final, desperate strike, the rogue Deathwalker's spear shattered, the force of the blow knocking it back. The red hue in its eyes dimmed, replaced by a flicker of recognition and regret. For a brief moment, the Deathwalker seemed to return to its original form, the corruption lifting like a shroud.

"Rye…" it whispered, its voice weak but clear. "I'm sorry. I couldn't—"

Before it could finish, the Deathwalker collapsed, its body disintegrating into the swirling sands. Rye stood over the spot where it had fallen, a mixture of anger and sadness coursing through him. Ammit's influence had taken yet another life, and he knew that the battle was far from over.

"You think you've found power?" Ammit snarled, her voice echoing through the funnel. "You are nothing compared to me!"

Rye raised the Ka sword, its blade gleaming with the combined energies of the grid and his own spirit. He could feel the darkness within the sword, the forbidden energy that had been locked away for centuries. It was a risk, a dangerous gamble that could easily corrupt him. But Rye knew that this was their only chance.

He channeled the energy into the sword, the blade glowing with a blinding light that cut through the swirling sands. The power surged through him, threatening to overwhelm his senses, but Rye held firm. He could feel the balance within him, a delicate harmony of light and darkness that allowed him to wield the sword without succumbing to its influence.

With a swift motion, Rye slashed through the air, unleashing a wave of energy that rippled through the funnel. The blast struck Ammit with a force that sent her reeling, her form flickering as the energy disrupted her chaotic powers.

For a moment, she seemed to lose her grip on the grid, her control over the funnel slipping as she struggled to maintain her form.

Rye pressed the advantage, moving with a speed and precision that defied the chaos around him. He struck again and again, each blow driving Ammit back, tearing through the layers of darkness that shielded her. Another rogue Deathwalker, still corrupted by Ammit's influence, tried to intervene, but Rye's attacks were relentless. He struck the Deathwalker down with a decisive blow, severing the last threads of corruption that bound it to Ammit's will.

As the Deathwalker crumbled to the sands, Rye turned his full attention to Ammit. She roared in defiance, summoning the last of her power in a final, desperate attack. But Rye was ready. He raised the Ka sword, channeling the forbidden energy into a single, concentrated strike. The blade cut through the air, slicing through Ammit's defenses and striking her core.

Ammit screamed, her form shattering as the energy tore through her. The funnel convulsed, the swirling sands collapsing inward as the grid's power was released. Rye watched as Ammit's form disintegrated, her chaotic energy dissipating into the air. For a moment, there was silence, the storm having finally run its course.

Rye floated above the ruins of the funnel, his breath steady as he surveyed the scene. He had done it. Ammit was defeated, her power broken. But as he looked at the Ka sword, still glowing with the dark energy he had unleashed,

Rye knew that the battle was far from over. The true enemy was still out there, lurking in the shadows, waiting for the right moment to strike.

Rye touched down on the sand, his new form shimmering in the fading light of the funnel. He looked at Mal and Ena, who had watched the transformation with a mix of awe and concern. They approached cautiously, unsure of what to make of their friend's new appearance.

"Rye," Mal said, his voice filled with a mix of relief and bewilderment. "What… what happened to you?"

Ena stepped closer, her eyes scanning Rye's skeletal form. "You've changed… but you're still you, right?"

Rye nodded, a faint smile crossing his face. "I'm still me. Just… more."

Ena reached out, playfully patting Rye on the head. "You've lost your hair, though," she said with a smirk.

Rye chuckled, manifesting his black hair with a thought. He shook his head, letting the strands fall back into place. "There. Better?"

They shared a brief, light-hearted moment, a welcome respite after the chaos of the battle. But the threat of what lay ahead loomed large, and Rye knew that there was still much to be done. The gods had yet to reveal themselves, and the true nature of the darkness they faced was still unknown.

Ammit, though momentarily weakened by Rye's strike, had not yet surrendered. Her fragmented form flickered at the center of the collapsed funnel, her eyes blazing with defiance. She drew herself up, the remnants of her chaotic energy coalescing around her like a dark shroud. The ground trembled beneath her as she let out a deafening roar, the sound resonating like thunder across the desert.

"You think you've won?" Ammit's voice, though distorted, was filled with venom. "You have only delayed the inevitable. I am chaos incarnate, and you cannot destroy what is eternal!"

Rye clenched the Ka sword, its blade still humming with the forbidden energy he had unleashed. He could feel the strain of wielding such power, the darkness within the sword threatening to pull him under. But he knew that this was their chance to end Ammit's reign once and for all. He glanced at Mal and Ena, who stood ready at his side, their resolve unwavering despite the odds.

"We need to finish this," Rye said, his voice steady but laced with urgency. "Ammit's still connected to the grid. If we don't sever her link completely, she'll keep coming back."

"We need to hit her where it hurts—disrupt her connection and break her control over the grid," said Ena.

Mal stepped forward, his winds swirling around him in a protective barrier. "I'll keep her distracted. You two focus on cutting off her power. Whatever it takes."

Rye tightened his grip on the Ka sword and took a deep breath. They had come this far together, and he knew that they had the strength to see it through. "Let's end this."

The three of them charged forward, diving into the fray as Ammit unleashed a torrent of chaotic energy. The ground split open, releasing serpentine creatures made of sand and flame that slithered toward them with terrifying speed. Mal, acting quickly, whipped up a cyclone that caught the creatures mid-charge, sending them spiraling into the sky, where they disintegrated in the swirling winds.

Ena launched beams of concentrated light at Ammit, each one aimed to disrupt the flow of energy that sustained her. The beams struck true, momentarily dispersing the dark aura around Ammit and causing her to recoil. But Ammit, ever resilient, retaliated with a blast of energy that sent shockwaves through the sand, knocking Ena back.

Rye pushed forward, using the Ka sword to deflect Ammit's attacks. Each clash of their powers sent sparks flying, illuminating the battlefield with bursts of light and shadow. Rye could feel the strain of maintaining the balance within the sword, the dark energy threatening to consume him. But he pressed on, knowing that he had to keep Ammit's attention focused on him.

Ammit's form flickered, her grip on the grid's energy weakening under the relentless assault. Sensing her vulnerability, Rye channeled a surge of power through the Ka sword, aiming for the heart of her connection. The blade cut through the air, slicing into the flow of energy that tethered Ammit to the grid. For a moment, the connection wavered, and Ammit let out a furious scream as the power slipped from her grasp.

But just as they seemed to gain the upper hand, Ammit roared in defiance, summoning her last reserves of strength. Her form solidified, and she lashed out with renewed ferocity, her movements erratic but fueled by pure rage. The ground beneath Rye cracked and shifted as Ammit's power tore through the earth, sending geysers of sand and molten rock into the air.

Mal struggled to maintain his balance, his wind barriers straining against the onslaught. "We're losing control! She's too strong-"

Before he could finish, a massive sand serpent burst from the ground, its jaws snapping at Mal with lightning speed. Mal dodged, barely avoiding the creature's fangs, but the effort left him off balance. Rye leaped into action, slashing at the serpent with the Ka sword. The blade cut through the creature's head, turning it to dust before it could strike again.

Back on her feet, Ena hurled another beam of light at Ammit, aiming to sever the last threads of her connection to the grid. But Ammit countered with a blast of dark energy, sending the beam scattering harmlessly into the sand. Ena gritted her teeth, refusing to back down as she pressed the attack.

Rye saw his chance. With Ammit's focus split between defending herself and maintaining her link to the grid, she was vulnerable. He poured all of his energy into the Ka sword, the blade glowing with an intense light that cut through the surrounding darkness. He charged forward; the sword raised high as he aimed for the center of Ammit's power.

Ammit, sensing the impending strike, tried to retreat, but the funnel's pull held her in place. Rye closed the distance, swinging the Ka sword in a powerful arc. The blade connected with a surge of energy, slicing through Ammit's core and severing her from the grid once and for all.

Ammit let out a final, anguished scream as her form disintegrated, the chaotic energy that had sustained her dissipating into the air. The funnel collapsed in on itself, the swirling sands falling away to reveal the scorched earth beneath. For a moment, all was still, the storm finally at rest.

Rye stood at the center of the battlefield, his breath heavy as he surveyed the remnants of their struggle. The Ka sword, its blade still glowing faintly, felt lighter in his hand, the dark energy within it finally subsiding. He turned to Mal and Ena, who were catching their breath, their expressions a mixture of exhaustion and relief.

"We did it," Mal said, his voice hoarse but triumphant. "Ammit's gone. We actually did it."

Ena nodded, her light powers dimming as she let out a long exhale. "It's over. We've stopped her."

But Rye, though relieved, couldn't shake the feeling that their victory was incomplete. As he looked at the Ka sword, he remembered the forbidden energy he had unleashed—a power that had come at a cost. The battle with Ammit was over, but the darkness they had faced was still out there, waiting for its chance to return.

Rye sheathed the Ka sword, the blade's glow fading as he turned his gaze to the horizon. The sun was setting, casting long shadows across the desert. The war for balance was far from over, and he knew that there were greater challenges yet to come.

As the last remnants of Ammit's chaotic form dissolved into the swirling sands, a brief, fragile silence fell over the battlefield. Rye, Mal, and Ena stood amidst the ruins of their struggle, the weight of their victory hanging heavily in the charged air. The ground was scorched, and the funnel that had once been a symbol of Ammit's power now lay in ruins, its energy dissipated.

But Rye's sense of unease only grew. The Ka sword, though subdued, still thrummed with residual dark energy— a reminder of the immense power they had unleashed. He knew they couldn't rest yet. Ammit's defeat, while significant, felt like only a prelude to a greater, looming threat.

The stillness was shattered by a sudden, violent tremor. The ground beneath them split open, and a fissure tore through the earth, radiating from the center of the collapsed funnel. From the depths of the chasm, a dark, ominous energy began to seep out, swirling like a black mist that coiled and writhed as if alive.

"What the hell is that?" Mal gasped, his eyes wide as he stepped back from the spreading darkness.

Ena's face paled, her light powers flickering in response to the presence of the new threat. "It's not over. There's something else… something worse."

Rye moved closer to the edge of the chasm, peering into the abyss. The energy emanating from the depths was unlike anything he had felt before—ancient, powerful, and filled with a malevolence that chilled him to his core. He could sense the presence of something far more dangerous than Ammit, lurking just beyond the veil of darkness.

Without warning, the air around them began to shimmer, and a series of figures materialized at the edge of the battlefield. Rye turned, his grip tightening on the Ka sword as he recognized the familiar forms of the ancient gods— Osiris, Horus, and others, their ethereal presences glowing with an otherworldly light.

Osiris, the leader of the divine assembly, said, "You have done well to defeat Ammit," he said, his voice resonating with the authority of ages. "But this battle was only a test— a prelude to what is to come."

Rye's eyes narrowed. "What's happening? What's down there?"

Osiris glanced at the chasm, his gaze hardening. "A darkness that predates even the gods—a force that seeks to unravel the balance of all realms. It has been waiting, biding its time, and now it stirs, awakened by the disruption of Ammit's power."

Horus, his eyes sharp and watchful, added, "Ammit was only a pawn, a distraction. The true enemy lies beneath, a force of chaos that seeks to consume all light and shadow, leaving nothing but void."

Rye felt a chill run through him. He had suspected that there was more to Ammit's influence, but the revelation that greater darkness was at play was more than he had anticipated. He looked at the gods, their forms flickering like distant stars in the twilight. They had intervened now, but their presence felt different—less authoritative, more uncertain.

From the shadows behind the gods, another figure emerged, drawing a sharp breath from Rye and his allies. Set, the god of chaos and once a sworn enemy of Osiris, stepped forward. His appearance was different from the last time they had seen him—his form less imposing, his eyes filled with a strange, reflective sorrow.

"Set?" Mal blurted, his confusion mirrored on Ena's face. "What's he doing here?"

Osiris placed a hand on Set's shoulder, a gesture of both restraint and acceptance. "Set has returned seeking redemption. He understands now that his actions have contributed to this greater threat. He has offered his aid in correcting the balance that he once sought to disrupt."

Set nodded solemnly. "I was blinded by my own desire for power, but I see now that what lies below is beyond any of us. It is a force that neither chaos nor order can control. It seeks to end all things."

Rye could feel the sincerity in Set's words, a stark contrast to the arrogance that had once defined the god of chaos. There was no longer a battle for dominance; they were united by a common enemy, one that threatened the very fabric of existence.

"We must act quickly," Osiris said, his tone urgent. "The darkness is spreading, feeding off the energy that was released during the battle. If it is not contained, it will consume everything in its path."

Rye stepped forward. "What do we need to do?"

Osiris turned to Rye, his expression unreadable. "You have already transformed once, but there is more to your journey. To confront this darkness, you must embrace both the light and shadow within you, truly become the balance that you wield with the Ka sword."

Rye looked down at the sword. He had fought so hard to maintain that balance, to keep the darkness at bay while wielding the light. But now, Osiris was asking him to go further, to fully embody the very concept of balance beyond any previous transformation.

Set stepped closer, his gaze intense. "Rye, you have become more than just a warrior. You are a bridge between worlds, between light and dark, life and death. That power is yours alone. You must descend into the chasm and face the source of this darkness. Only then can you hope to contain it."

Rye nodded, the weight of his task settling over him like a mantle. He knew that this was the next step in his journey—a descent into the unknown, a confrontation with a force that defied all boundaries. But he was not afraid. He had faced chaos before and emerged stronger, and he would do so again.

Mal and Ena stepped forward, their expressions fierce with determination. "We're coming with you," Mal said firmly. "We've come this far together, and we're not leaving you to face this alone."

Ena nodded in agreement, her light powers sparking in anticipation. "We'll fight by your side, whatever comes."

Rye smiled, grateful for their unwavering support. "Thank you. I couldn't do this without you."

Osiris raised his hand, and a pathway of light appeared, leading down into the chasm. The gods formed a protective circle around the opening, their powers combining to create a barrier that would hold back the darkness for as long as possible.

"Go now," Osiris urged. "The darkness will not wait, and neither should you."

Rye, Mal, and Ena exchanged determined looks before stepping onto the path. They descended into the chasm, the oppressive darkness growing thicker with every step. The light from the gods above flickered but held, guiding them deeper into the unknown.

As they reached the bottom, the true source of the darkness came into view—a swirling mass of shadow and void pulsing with an unearthly energy. Rye could feel its presence pressing against him, a force that sought to devour everything it touched.

This was it—the final confrontation, the moment that would determine the fate of all realms. Rye knew that he would have to push beyond his limits to draw upon the deepest reserves of his power and courage. He glanced at Mal and Ena, who stood ready beside him, their faces set with unwavering resolve.

Together, they faced the darkness, their combined strength a beacon of hope in the midst of the abyss. Rye raised the Ka sword, preparing to strike the first blow. The battle was far from over, but they were ready to meet it head-on, united in their purpose.

Rye, Mal, and Ena stood at the base of the chasm, their surroundings a swirling vortex of darkness and raw, untamed energy. The air was thick with the oppressive weight of the malevolent force they had come to confront, its presence almost tangible as it pressed against their senses. In the heart of the abyss, the true source of the ancient darkness loomed—a massive, undulating mass of shadows pulsating with a rhythm that seemed to echo from the dawn of time itself.

The blade had been their beacon through countless battles, a symbol of balance and resilience. But now, facing the abyss, even the Ka sword seemed diminished, its light struggling against the consuming void.

"This is it," Rye said, his voice steady despite the tension that gripped him. "The darkness that even the gods fear. It's stronger than anything we've faced."

Mal nodded, his winds swirling protectively around them. "Then we hit it with everything we've got. No holding back."

Ena stepped forward, her light powers flaring as she raised her hands. "We're with you, Rye. Whatever happens, we face it together."

As they prepared to strike, a figure began to materialize within the darkness—a familiar form that sent a shiver through the group. Ammit, though defeated and subdued, emerged from the shadows, her presence more subdued but still potent. Her eyes, no longer blazing with unchecked fury, now held a strange clarity as if the shattering of her chaotic form had brought a moment of understanding.

"Ammit?" Rye asked, his grip on the Ka sword tightening as he watched her approach. "What are you doing here?"

Ammit's voice, though still echoing with the remnants of her power, carried a tone of warning. "I am not your enemy now, Rye. Not in this place, where true darkness resides."

She gestured toward the pulsating mass of shadows, her expression a mix of fear and resignation. "This is the ancient void, a darkness that existed long before any of us. It feeds on the energy of gods and mortals alike, consuming all in its path. Even I, in my most chaotic form, was but a tool to this force."

Rye's eyes narrowed as he absorbed her words. He had always known that their battles were part of a larger struggle, but hearing it from Ammit herself gave him pause. The enemy they faced was not just a being of chaos—it was the embodiment of entropy, an ancient hunger that sought to unmake the very fabric of reality.

"Why warn us now?" Ena asked, her light flickering uncertainly. "You've fought against us at every turn. What changed?"

Ammit looked at Ena, a shadow of regret crossing her features. "When Rye severed my link to the grid, he did more than just defeat me. He freed me from the grasp of this void. For the first time, I see the futility of fighting against the balance that the gods uphold. But this force—" she gestured again to the darkness—"it seeks to end all things, balance included."

Rye considered her words, his mind racing as he tried to form a plan. The Ka sword thrummed with anticipation, sensing the nearness of its ultimate test. "So what do we do?" he asked, glancing at his companions. "We can't just attack it blindly. We need to find a way to contain it, or at least weaken it."

Ammit's gaze was on the abyss. "The darkness can be bound, but it requires more than just brute strength. It demands sacrifice and a deep understanding of what it means to truly balance light and shadow."

Rye looked at her, then at the swirling void that lay ahead. He knew that they couldn't afford to hesitate. Every second they spent in the presence of the abyss felt like a countdown to the end of all things. He turned to Mal and Ena, their faces set with determination despite the daunting task before them.

He stepped closer to the edge of the abyss, the Ka sword held before him. He could feel the darkness pushing back, a force that threatened to pull him in, to strip away all that he was. But he also felt the presence of his friends beside him, their unwavering support giving him the strength to face the void.

Rye raised the Ka sword high, the blade glowing with a brilliant light that cut through the darkness. He focused on the balance within the sword, drawing on the harmony of light and shadow that he had fought so hard to maintain. The blade responded, its glow intensifying as it resonated with the energy of the abyss.

Ammit watched. "The void will try to consume you. If you let it in, even for a moment, it will take everything."

Rye stepped forward, bringing the Ka sword down in a sweeping arc that sliced through the void. The blade connected with the shadows, and for a moment, the abyss recoiled, its form shuddering under the impact.

A surge of energy exploded from the point of contact, sending shockwaves rippling through the chasm. Rye gritted his teeth, holding the sword steady as the darkness fought back, trying to overwhelm him. The void pushed against him, its presence a suffocating weight that threatened to pull him under.

But Rye held firm, drawing on the balance within the Ka sword and within himself. He could feel the energy of the sword intertwining with the void, not to destroy but to contain. It was a delicate dance, a test of will and endurance that stretched him to his limits.

The abyss roared in defiance, but the Ka sword's light did not falter. Inch by inch, Rye pushed back, forcing the darkness into a more contained form. The shadows writhed and twisted, but they could not break free from the binding power of the sword.

Finally, with a final, shuddering cry, the void collapsed inward, the darkness folding in on itself as it was sealed within the confines of the Ka sword's light. The chasm fell silent, the pulsating mass of shadows reduced to a faint, flickering glow that hovered at the edge of existence.

Rye lowered the Ka sword, his breath ragged but victorious. The void was contained, at least for now; its threat diminished but not entirely gone. He knew that they had won a crucial battle, but the war for balance would continue. The ancient darkness, though subdued, would always be waiting, lurking just beyond the boundaries of light and shadow.

Osiris and the other gods descended into the chasm, their expressions solemn but filled with quiet respect for the warriors who had faced the abyss and survived. Set approached Rye, his gaze reflective as he looked at the Ka sword.

"You did it," Set said quietly. "You faced the void and held your ground. Not many can say that."

Rye nodded, his eyes still fixed on the faint glow of the contained darkness. "We did what we had to. But this isn't over. Not yet."

Osiris stepped forward, his presence commanding as he addressed the group. "Rye, you have proven yourself to be a true champion of balance. But remember, the void is never truly defeated. It is only ever held at bay. Your journey is far from complete."

Rye sheathed the Ka sword, its glow dimming as it settled into its dormant state. He knew that Osiris was right. The battle against chaos and darkness was an ongoing struggle, one that required constant vigilance and the strength to face the unknown.

As the gods prepared to depart, Ammit lingered, her form still flickering with the remnants of her chaotic nature. She looked at Rye, her expression one of solemn gratitude.

"You spared me," she said softly. "When you had every reason to destroy me, you chose balance instead. For that, I thank you."

Rye nodded, a faint smile crossing his face. "Everyone deserves a chance to find their place. Even those who have walked in shadow."

With a final nod, Ammit faded into the shadows, her form dissolving as she returned to the realms beyond. Rye, Mal, and Ena watched her go, the chasm finally quiet after the storm of battle.

But as they turned to leave, the ground rumbled once more, a faint tremor that sent a ripple through the sands. Rye paused, glancing back at the faint glow of the contained void. It was a reminder that their victory, while significant, was only a temporary reprieve.

The true enemy still lurked in the shadows, biding its time. And Rye knew that when it returned, they would need to be ready.